न हि ज्ञानेन सदृशं पवित्रमिह विद्यते ।
तत्स्वयं योगसंसिद्धः कालेनात्मनि विन्दति ।।

In this world, there is nothing so purifying as knowledge.
One who is perfected in understanding finds it within
oneself in due course of time.

(Bhagavad Gita, 4:38)

DR MARK

CASEBOOK OF A PARANORMAL INVESTIGATOR

DR MARK

CASEBOOK OF A PARANORMAL INVESTIGATOR

YADU VIJAYAKRISHNAN

Quantic books

Quantic books

ENGLISH

DR MARK: CASEBOOK OF A PARANORMAL INVESTIGATOR

(Novel)

Yadu Vijayakrishnan

Published by
Quantic Creatives Private Limited.
Corporate Office: Quantic Nexus
TC 22/2459, SRL-A 68, Sankar Road, Sasthamangalam,
Thiruvananthapuram, Kerala 695010
Tel: 8289816366 | 8590011447
www.quanticcreatives.in

First published in 2026

Layout: Qlife Infotech

Cover Design and Layout by Yadu Vijayakrishnan

ISBN: 978-81-986512-0-4

Price: ₹ 349.00

Contents

CONTENT NOTE

This book explores themes of fear, belief, psychological distress and death. Certain scenes depict emotionally intense situations and discuss mental health, grief and the consequences of manipulation, misinformation and superstition. These elements are handled without graphic detail and within a rational, investigative framework.

Readers who are sensitive to such themes may wish to proceed at their own pace.

CHAPTER ONE

Paranormal Human Combustion

It was noon. The sun blazed directly overhead, baking the Thiruvananthapuram District Court. The crowd outside had swelled far beyond the usual, spilling onto the roads. Reporters from every major news outlet jostled for position with their lenses tracking every move. The air buzzed with anticipation. The accused was none other than a controversial political figure, a Member of Legislative Assembly.

The news came from inside. The politician, Anwar, was found not guilty of the rape and murder of a 13-year-old girl. When Anwar came out of the building, his followers greeted him with slogans. They also prevented the reporters and cameramen from going near him.

Anwar's driver rushed to the black SUV and opened the passenger door for him to get in. He closed the door and as the driver rushed to get in his driver's seat, he couldn't open the door.

Anwar saw the car getting closed from inside. The driver felt an electric shock when he tried to open the door once again. He wasn't sure what was happening.

The politician watched in horror as the car started on its own, smoke pouring from the AC ducts. He yanked at the doors, but the vehicle seemed alive, resisting him at every turn. His followers all were stunned by electric shock when they tried to open the door to let him out. They all stayed back.

Then, the airbags deployed explosively, filling the cabin with a dense mist. Anwar was drenched in some strange liquid, slipping and coughing, panic overtook him.

'Somebody open the door, help me!' he cried.

One of his followers came running with a 2-foot iron rod and broke open the glass windows. Anwar, with his big body, struggled to get out of the car from the window. After some painful minutes, he fell to the ground, relieved.

The news reporters were covering the events from afar with utmost excitement. They were giving their own commentaries.

But, something out of the ordinary happened that silenced everyone.

Anwar began screaming and crying in anguish. Nobody knew why.

But then, they saw his skin getting red. His flesh blistered as if seared alive. The air was filled with a pungent, burning smell.

Two of his followers rushed to him to help but they retreated after experiencing some sort of burning sensation.

Anwar screamed as his flesh seemed to burn without any fire. Some thought the harsh sun itself is burning him. While some others thought he was being cursed. Something paranormal had happened.

The murmurs swelled into panic as others tried to approach, only to recoil from invisible shocks. Hands went up to shield faces. The police were helpless as well. Nobody had any idea what was happening.

People stumbled backward, bumping into one another with their eyes wide with disbelief. Some fell to their knees. Others fumbled with their phones, unable to comprehend what they were capturing. The twenty or thirty seconds of agony stretched into something that felt like an hour. Only then did a fire finally reveal itself, crawling across his clothes in sudden, unmistakable flames.

Then Anwar collapsed to the ground like grilled pork.

Some vomited while some screamed. No one dared approach the body. The police were reduced to be just stunned observers. They guarded the perimeter and trying futilely to control the hysteria.

The visuals telecasted and streamed live and became viral instantly. People wanted answers. This wasn't just a random person.

For most, it was perhaps the first time something paranormal has happened to someone famous, that too in broad daylight, that too being witnessed by hundreds.

Anwar's body was taken away. The City Commissioner, Vikram IPS was summoned by the Chief Minister.

'What the hell happened? An MLA of our coalition is dead by a mysterious force in broad daylight!' the CM barked. 'Don't waste time on formalities. We want answers.'

'Yes, sir,' replied Vikram, the bulky man with thick moustache was expecting the CM's anger.

'And…make sure the public gets a clear explanation of what happened,' said the CM. 'I don't want them to be believing the supernaturals again.'

As soon as Vikram exited the CM's office, he was briefed by his subordinates that the forensic team is already at the site.

'Let them do their job,' said Vikram. 'But to convince the

public about what really had happened, I need him.'

'Who?' asked his subordinate officer.

*

'Hello, everyone! Once again, welcome to Chai with Satyajit! I'm your host, Satyajit and today we have with us a very special guest. Neuro-behavioural specialist and consultant psychiatrist to the police, Dr Markandeyan,' Satyajit announced with his usual enthusiasm, looking straight into the camera.

Across the table, Dr Markandeyan offered a polite smile and a small wave to the camera. He cut a calm, composed figure. A bearded man in his early forties with the quiet confidence of someone who had spent years studying the human mind and chemistry. His face was lean, framed by neatly trimmed beard. A pair of aviator-framed spectacles rested lightly on the bridge of his nose. His hair tousled despite his attempts to flatten it before the show. He wore a simple cotton shirt, sleeves rolled up just enough to show a tattoo ॐ. A watch with a worn leather strap hugged his left wrist. It was functional, not fashionable, much like the man himself.

'So, Dr Markandeyan -'

'You can call me Mark,' he interrupted with a faint smile.

'Alright then, Dr Mark,' said Satyajit. 'Recently, you've faced quite a lot of criticism online for your remarks on religion. What would you like to say to your critics?'

Mark's phone had been vibrating relentlessly for the past five minutes. He tried to ignore it at first, but the screen kept lighting up beside his cup of tea.

'Ah, sorry, could I just check my phone for a moment? I think there's some sort of emergency,' he asked.

Satyajit frowned slightly but gestured to the camera crew with a scissor-like motion, signalling them to stop recording.

Mark glanced at the phone. Ten missed calls from

Commissioner Vikram. Just as he was about to return the call, it started buzzing again. He picked up immediately.

'Mark, didn't you see the news?' came Vikram's urgent voice.

'No. What's going on?'

'Come to my office right now. I've sent you a few links, check them on the way.'

'Alright,' said Mark, already rising from his chair.

He turned to Satyajit. 'I'm really sorry, Satyajit. Something urgent came up. I'll have to leave.'

'It's alright, we can continue another day,' replied Satyajit, managing a disappointed smile.

Mark hurried out of the studio. In the lobby, Ashok was waiting, scrolling through his phone.

'That was quick,' said Ashok, pocketing his mobile. 'Anyways, you wouldn't believe what was happening.'

'Had to cancel the shoot,' Mark replied, walking briskly towards the exit. 'Vikram called. We need to get to the commissioner's office immediately.'

'I knew they will call you for this,' said Ashok while walking to the car.

As Ashok drove through the midday traffic, Mark opened the links that Vikram had sent. One after another, news clips, live broadcasts and unsteady phone recordings appeared on the screen. The comments beneath them were already flooding in.

It's a curse!

He was damned!

This is divine justice!

This is Spontaneous Human Combustion!

God has punished him!

This is the devil's doing!

Ashok glanced sideways, reading Mark's expression.

'Reading the comments, are you?'

'Yes,' Mark replied. 'I was hoping someone among the public might offer a rational observation. But I suppose that was too much to expect. People still cling to sorcery and superstition.'

'What do you think the explanation may be?' Ashok asked.

'I cannot say anything definitive without examining the body,' Mark answered. 'But at first glance, it might appear like a high-voltage electrocution triggered by the vehicle itself.'

'Ah, case solved already by the great Dr Mark!' Ashok said with theatrical enthusiasm.

Mark's expression changed immediately. He propped back, thoughtful.

'No. This is definitely not electrocution,' he said.

'Case open again,' Ashok murmured, amused. 'What makes you rule it out?'

'Electrocution is instantaneous,' Mark explained. 'The moment the body contacts the electrical source, the reaction is violent and immediate. In Anwar's case, the suffering continued for almost a minute even after he escaped the vehicle. There was no visible contact with any power source.'

'Maybe it was something in his clothes,' Ashok added. 'A mobile phone or a device exploding, perhaps?'

Mark shook his head. 'If it had been a mobile phone, we would have seen the explosion itself. In fact, the closest parallel is the Mossad operation in Lebanon and Syria. Israel remotely detonated thousands of modified pagers carried by terrorists. Every single one of those devices exploded in an instant. The reaction was immediate, bright flash, fragmentation and collapse. It was swift and unmistakable.'

He paused, recalling the images.

'But this,' he continued, 'is nothing like that. Anwar was not struck by a sudden blast. He endured a slow, progressive burn. That is entirely different in character and mechanism.'

Ashok acknowledged it silently.

'Right… that makes sense. Anyway, we've reached.'

Mark stepped out of the vehicle, still deep in thought.

'I will need to examine the evidence more closely before I draw any conclusion,' he said, closing the door behind him.

Mark stepped into Vikram's office. The room was already occupied by other police officers. They stood in tense clusters with files in their hands. The atmosphere was tense as though the entire department were holding its breath.

Vikram looked up the moment Mark entered.

'Hope you watched the videos I sent,' he said. 'Any idea what caused the death?'

Mark took a breath. He could still see Anwar's distorted face on the screen with the inexplicable burns.

'There are multiple possibilities,' he replied. 'But a paranormal activity isn't one of them.'

A faint murmur swept through the officers.

'I thought as much,' Vikram said, leaning back in his chair. 'But the pressure is mounting. We need an explanation and we need it fast. The public is in a frenzy and the politicians are feeding on it. The media is treating it like divine punishment.'

'Has the autopsy been completed? I'll need the reports.' Mark asked.

'It's underway,' Vikram said. 'They expect to finish by evening. If you prefer, you can visit the lab yourself and speak directly with the doctor and forensic experts.'

'I will,' Mark said.

'What about the car?' he asked.

'You need a vehicle arranged for the lab?' Vikram frowned.

'No,' Mark said evenly. 'I meant Anwar's car.'

'Ah.' Vikram straightened. 'It's in our custody. Secured in the police motor pool.'

Mark felt a spark of clarity, a fragment of the puzzle aligning in his mind.

'I suspect a cybercrime element here,' he said. The officers exchanged glances. 'The vehicle's behaviour was unnatural, self-locking, ignition without input, electrical discharges. These aren't coincidences. Someone could have manipulated the car from outside.'

The room grew quieter.

'Assign a cyber expert to the SUV,' Mark continued. 'I want a full diagnostic, software logs, recent updates, any remote-access signatures. I'll head there first. The car must be examined before the autopsy results come in. The two sets of data will complement each other.'

Vikram gave a decisive assent.

'Consider it done. I'll have the cyber unit meet you there within the hour.'

'Good,' Mark said, turning toward the door. 'The truth is in that vehicle. Whatever happened to Anwar didn't start with him, it started with the machine.'

Just then, a young officer seated before a laptop shot to his feet. His chair scraped loudly across the floor.

'Sir… you may want to see this,' he said. 'A video has posted online claiming to give a definite explanation for Anwar's death. It's going viral…millions of views already.'

Vikram exchanged a weary glance with Mark.

'Play it on the big screen,' he instructed.

The officer connected the laptop and within seconds the large display flickered to life.

The banner flashed *KeralaNewsFirst365*.

Then the video appeared.

A field reporter thrust a microphone toward a man who looked as though he had stepped out of a medieval tale, someone who belonged to desert bazaars or cramped mystical tents in the 600s CE.

The stranger had a pronounced prayer bump on his forehead. His beard was orange and curled tightly, yet he wore no moustache. His eyes were dull and lifeless like a dead fish. A green shawl hung loosely over his shoulders. He appeared to be around fifty.

A subtitle appeared at the bottom of the screen:

Rashid Parambilmana.

Mark closed his eyes briefly and pressed his fingers to his forehead.

'Oh God… this man again,' he muttered.

Vikram glanced at him. 'You know him?'

'Unfortunately,' Mark replied. 'He pops up during every public tragedy claiming supernatural intervention. People eat it up.'

On screen, Rashid raised a finger solemnly.

'We have all witnessed the live video of what happened to the MLA,' he declared, his tone theatrical, almost triumphant. 'I can say without the slightest doubt, black magic is behind this. MLA Anwar had many enemies in politics. And certain Hindutva elements wanted him removed. It is clear to me that someone from that side has invoked a powerful sorcery… a ritual meant to kill him in this paranormal manner.'

The room erupted in irritated murmurs. A few officers shook their heads.

Mark exhaled sharply.

'I don't wanna watch this anymore,' he said, stepping back. 'Neither should you guys.' His tone was calm but edged with frustration. He turned to Vikram. 'I'll be at the motor pool. The car needs to be examined before more superstition spreads.'

Vikram nodded. 'One of my men will take you.'

Mark walked out of the room.

Vikram remained in front of the large screen. Rashid's voice still echoed in the room like curses.

'…powerful sorcery… invoked against a political figure… signs of a curse…'

An officer muted the video.

The room felt colder now. Even seasoned officers looked unsettled, not because they believed Rashid, but because millions of the public did.

'Sir,' one officer whispered, 'what if people who gathered outside court demanding a divine punishment for Anwar had caused some sort of paranormal energy built up? Maybe it's something like that.'

Vikram clenched his jaw.

'If the world worked like that then there is no need for police or judiciary,' said Vikram.

He looked through the glass window, watching Mark disappear into the courtyard below.

Outside, a lean officer in uniform was waiting for Mark.

'Sir, the commissioner told me to take you to the motor pool,' he said. 'I'm Sandeep.'

Mark nodded and followed him through the courtyard. As they walked, Mark could not shake the image of Anwar's final moments, the slow agony, the desperate cries, the inexplicable burns.

'Sir,' Sandeep said softly as they approached the parking zone, 'I was there… at the court. When it happened.'

Mark slowed down. 'You saw it directly?'

'Yes. I was part of the security team. Everything happened so fast… yet it felt so long. People kept screaming. I've never seen a man burn without fire.' His words trembled slightly.

Mark placed a hand on his shoulder. 'It must have been traumatic. But what you saw will help us. Anything unusual… anything at all…might be important.'

Sandeep drew a steadying breath.

They reached the motor pool. Anwar's black SUV stood isolated in the corner, surrounded by yellow police tape. Even from a distance, Mark felt an instinctive unease. It was the same vehicle he had watched over and over on the videos … the locked doors, the smoke, the spasms, the invisible shocks.

'Has anyone touched it?' Mark asked.

'No, sir. Only the forensic team looked at the exterior. They didn't open the doors.'

Mark stared at the vehicle.

'Good. We need everything exactly as it was.'

Just then, a young spectacled man with a laptop bag approached them.

'Cyber Cell,' he said, adjusting his glasses. 'Name's Neeraj. The commissioner said you wanted a full sweep.'

'Yes,' said Mark. 'This seems to be the latest model of a SmartCar with access to internet and stuffs. Please check every log, every remote command, every unexplained signal.'

Neeraj acknowledged the instruction and got to work, carefully unlocking the car with insulated gloves. As he opened the door, a faint chemical odour drifted out, strong, but unnervingly sterile, like laboratory fumes masked by air freshener.

Mark leaned forward.

The AC vents appeared slightly discoloured.

'Sir,' Neeraj said quietly, 'the last recorded ignition command… it wasn't from the key.'

Mark looked up sharply.

'Then where did it come from?'

Neeraj's fingers flew across his keyboard.

'A remote access point. Unauthorised. Masked.'

'Meaning?' Sandeep asked, visibly unsettled.

'Meaning someone hijacked the vehicle online,' replied

Mark.

He paused, swallowing the fact that now seemed impossible to deny.

'This wasn't an accident. Someone planned this… down to the second.'

Sandeep stared at the SUV, fear quietly rising in his eyes.

'How can anyone even do that?'

Mark looked at him with a chilling certainty.

'Just how someone can remotely connect your Wi-Fi mouse or smartwatch, someone has connected the admin access to the car,' replied Neeraj.

'And that person have locked the car from inside and turned the engine on,' added Mark.

Mark opened the back door where the glass was shattered. A faint chemical smell drifted out. He went to the front and crouched near the dashboard to examine the AC vents closely.

The plastic edges around the slats were warped, slightly melted, but not from heat alone. The surface shimmered faintly.

Mark raised his finger and gently touched the vent. The residue smelt faintly sweet. The smell was too subtle for the untrained nose, but unmistakable to him.

'Methanol…' Mark stepped back, surveying the interior again. 'Neeraj, run a full diagnostic on the airbag deployment system. I need to know whether someone tampered with it.'

Neeraj went to work immediately, connecting his tools. 'Already on it, sir.'

Mark tilted into the car again, this time focusing on the edges of the seat fabric. Burn patterns… micro-scorch marks… chemical pitting…

The pieces were lining up like shards of glass.

'Sir… you were right.' Neeraj's voice cut through the stale air of the garage.

Mark turned sharply. The glow of Neeraj's laptop reflected in his anxious eyes.

'The hacker triggered the airbags,' Neeraj continued, breathless. 'The deployment wasn't mechanical. It was remotely fired.'

A spark flickered in Mark's expression.

He grabbed his phone and dialled Commissioner Vikram.

'Vikram,' he said the moment the call connected, 'I'll crack this by tonight. Send the forensic team here immediately. There's something they need to check. I'll brief Sandeep.'

He ended the call and turned to the two young officers.

'I'm heading to the lab,' Mark said. 'I've got almost everything I need from the vehicle. Except one thing.'

'What's that, sir?' Sandeep asked.

'Tell the forensic team to look for canisters, small, concealed, any kind, connected to the airbags.'

Sandeep and Neeraj nodded eagerly.

The drive to the medical centre was quick, tense and silent. Ashok kept glancing at Mark without asking anything.

Inside the lab, the world shifted.

The bright, cold lights hummed above like a sterile, artificial sky. The smell of antiseptic was sharp.

Dr. Srikant waited by the entrance of the post-mortem chamber. Even for a man desensitised by years of cutting open corpses, he looked disturbed.

'Mark… I was expecting you,' he said quietly. 'The body is inside.'

They walked in.

Anwar's remains lay under a white sheet. The scars twisted across his skin like melted wax. It was a sight that momentarily made the room colder.

'We assumed electrocution at first,' Srikant said, rubbing his temples. 'But the injuries do not match.'

'I ruled that out after watching the footage,' Mark murmured, stepping closer. The smell of burnt flesh still clung faintly to the remains.

'Exactly,' Srikant said, pointing to the blistering. 'The burns are diffuse. Layered. Not electrical. This is chemical. Deliberate.'

'Methanol?' Mark asked.

Srikant's head snapped up.

'You noticed it too?'

Mark nodded.

'Traces inside the car. Enough to coat skin. Enough to burn on exposure.' Mark paused. 'I think I understand what caused the reaction.'

Srikant sighed with visible relief. 'I'm glad my part is nearly done. Now I'm waiting for you to tell me how methanol appeared from nowhere.'

'You won't have to wait long,' Mark said, turning away. 'The answers are already forming.'

As Mark left the lab, something in the corridor halted him. The faint smell of antiseptic, the cold tiles beneath his feet, the hum of fluorescent lights. All felt familiar.

A memory returned, uninvited.

A hospital corridor.

A stretcher.

His wife's still face beneath a white sheet.

The sound of a baby crying.

He had stood there alone, years ago, a ring still on his finger, unable to process the suddenness of loss. Nothing supernatural. Nothing intentional. Just an avoidable tragedy masked as unfortunate fate.

The sound of the crying baby grew louder and louder.

The crying stopped. Or did it transition to his phone's ringtone.

Yes, it was Dr Mark's phone buzzing violently.

Sandeep.

'Sir,' Sandeep said, voice tight with adrenaline, 'the forensic team found something inside the AC ducts. Hidden attachments… metallic, cylindrical. They're definitely canisters.'

Mark closed his eyes briefly. He was not surprised.

'Good work. I'm coming. Wait for me at the police headquarters.'

By the time Mark and Ashok reached the headquarters, the place had transformed into chaos. Dozens of journalists swarmed the entrance, waving mics, phones and cameras like desperate birds demanding food.

Mark stepped out of the car, preparing to wedge through the crowd, when someone called his name sharply.

'Dr Mark!'

He turned.

Jyolsna pushed through the reporters, moving with the ease of someone who had fought many such battles. Her press ID hung from her neck and her hair pulled back.

'You're investigating this?' she asked, her breath already quick from the rush.

'Something supernatural and paranormal happened,' Mark said dryly. 'So, obviously, it ends up on my table.'

Jyolsna gave a faint, knowing smile. 'Then I'm sure you'll arrive at a logical explanation soon enough.'

'That's the plan,' Mark said. 'I strive for a world where people don't need investigators like me to tell them a curse isn't behind every tragedy.' His voice softened slightly. 'Until then, I suppose I have to keep debunking wild claims.'

'You're right,' she said, stepping aside to let him pass. 'And we need more voices like yours right now.'

Mark nodded and continued toward the building. The

noise of the crowd swelled behind him.

State Police Chief Sanjeev Kumar IPS, tall and broad-shouldered, rested his hands on the table with the air of a man who had seen both crime and politics.

Beside him stood the stiff-faced Inspector General, unblinking with an expression carved in stone.

Commissioner Vikram waited near the window, arms folded.

Neeraj, Sandeep and the forensic team stood at one end of the room, laptops open, metallic equipment cases on the floor beside them.

When Mark entered, the room turned.

'Dr Markandeyan,' the State Police Chief said, voice booming with forced warmth. 'Long time. How are you? Still hunting ghosts and demons?'

Mark allowed a faint smile.

'Yes, sir. And like always, they turn out to be humans.'

Sanjeev chuckled, a low sound that didn't touch his eyes.

'Exactly. You're a busy man now. Consultant Psychiatrist, Neuro-Behavioural Specialist, our unofficial "paranormal troubleshooter". Formerly tied to that mental-health institute… or was it a defence research wing?' He waved his hand dismissively. 'Either way, we don't pull you in unless there was a high profile politician as a victim.'

'I would've come even without your call. The superstition spreading outside is far more dangerous than the crime itself,' said Mark.

Sanjeev signalled his approval.

'Then let's get to it. What have you got?'

Dr Markandeyan explained the chain of events. His voice remained steady.

As he spoke, officers veered in. It appeared as though they were watching a movie. Dr Mark explained chemistry and technology with ease.

When Mark finished, silence settled.

Commissioner Vikram finally broke it.

'So who's behind this?'

Mark folded his hands.

'My job was to determine how he died. Not who killed him. That falls on Kerala Police. You'll have to follow the cyber trail embedded in the car's system.'

'You've done more than enough, Dr Mark. We owe you.' Sanjeev said gravely.

Mark hesitated, then spoke.

'I have one question. In the court case... does the murdered girl have any tech-savvy relative? Someone who might seek revenge?'

'No. She grew up in an orphanage. No parents. No cousins. Nothing.' Vikram shook his head. 'The only person who truly cared for her...or her soul...was the investigating officer - Maya.'

'Where is she now?' Mark asked.

Sanjeev and Vikram exchanged looks - political looks, heavy with the unsaid.

'Transferred,' Vikram said finally. 'Far edges of Wayanad. After she named Anwar as prime suspect. The case was reassigned, then quietly closed.'

Mark felt a coldness settle in his stomach.

Politics. Again.

Before he could speak, Sanjeev cut in sharply.

'Dr Markandeyan, there is... one more favour.'

'Tell me.' Mark straightened.

'At tomorrow's press conference, you must speak. We'll be there, but it must come from you. You're the face of logic. People trust you more than the uniform. If we explain the case, half the state will call it a cover-up. If you explain it, they'll listen.'

Mark took a breath.

'Alright. I'll do it.'

'Good. Then let's prepare for tomorrow,' he said, closing the file with a decisive thud.

Mark's house stood tucked away in a quiet residential pocket of Thiruvananthapuram. Built in the distinctive style Larry Baker had popularised decades ago, the structure looked almost sculpted out of shadow and geometry. At night, it felt alive.

The house rose two storeys high, a collage of exposed laterite stone and smooth timber panels, caught stray moonlight at different angles. Long vertical slits replaced traditional windows, glowing faintly like watchful eyes.

The ceiling sloped unevenly with Larry Baker's trademark "slant-roof asymmetry", allowing heat to rise and breeze to travel. Even at night, the house held a subtle nocturnal coolness.

Mark's study was tucked into one of the offsets of the split-level floor, separated from the living room by a half-wall and a narrow flight of floating wooden steps. The study light spilled out in a soft amber pool, illuminating the railings and catching the edges of books piled carelessly on the desk.

Everything about the house reflected Mark himself - logical, functional, minimalistic, yet holding a quiet emotional weight in its silence.

From the outside, it looked like an architectural statement. From the inside, it felt like a sanctuary.

That night, Mark had a visitor at home.

'Brother,' he said, stepping aside. 'Come in.'

Vishwamitran entered with the unmistakable shuffle of a man whose belly arrived a few seconds before the rest of him. He was the opposite of Mark, thick moustache, rounded face, pot-bellied, with the slightly flushed look of someone who had spent too many years surrounded by cases of liquor.

He held up a bottle like a trophy.

'Here. Something for you.'

Mark raised an eyebrow. 'Straight from work, I presume?'

'Of course,' Vishwamitran grinned. 'One of the perks of working in the Beverages Corporation, hm? Do you know - this Onam, the employees of our department got the highest bonus in the whole state.'

'Not surprising,' Mark said, taking the bottle. 'The liquor department is the most profitable arm of the government.'

'Exactly,' his brother said, puffing his chest out. 'We practically carry the state on our shoulders.'

Mark set the bottle on the table.

'So, why the unlikely visit? Had dinner?' Mark asked.

'Ate at home,' Vishwamitran said. He sat down slowly. 'I wanted to… tell you something personally.'

'Yes, brother. Tell me.'

There was a long pause.

'You know how me, mom and dad pushed you for civil service exams?' Vishwamitran finally said. 'You were a walking encyclopaedia. You still are. You could've been an IAS officer with your eyes closed. A government job… security… respect… perks…'

Mark rubbed his forehead.

'Not now, brother. Please. We've had this conversation thousand times.'

'You've put your knowledge to waste,' Vishwamitran muttered.

Mark leaned back, exhaling. 'I'm pretty sure I'm using it for something useful. For the society, at least.'

Vishwamitran sighed.

'Anyway, I didn't come here to rewrite your career. I came

because… I saw the news.'

'About the case?' Mark's shoulders eased slightly.

'Yes, about that MLA's death,' Vishwamitran said. 'And that the police are consulting you. That man… he was a controversial figure. You getting involved with him… even after his death… isn't something to take lightly.'

Mark studied his brother's face.

'You always need the government on your side no matter which political party is ruling the state,' Vishwamitran continued. 'If you've found something that could… trouble you later, better to step away. These political types… they don't forget.'

Mark offered a small, reassuring smile.

'I'm not in any danger, brother. Don't worry.'

Vishwamitran stood up slowly.

'Alright then,' he said finally. 'I'm leaving. Take care. And… be careful, son.'

He placed a hand briefly on Mark's shoulder before walking out.

Mark took his time with dinner, eating in the quiet rhythm of a man whose mind was elsewhere. When he finally finished and washed the dishes, the clatter of steel against the sink echoed through the empty house.

He switched off the kitchen light and walked slowly toward his bedroom.

The corridor was dim, lit only by a single wall lamp, its glow pooling softly on the framed photographs lining the passage.

He paused.

There they were - captured moments from a decade ago.

A younger Mark, smiling without caution. And beside him, his wife… her eyes bright, her laughter frozen in time, a warmth the world could no longer give him.

He traced a finger lightly across the glass.

Ten years since the wedding.

Ten years since he had walked beside her.

Ten years since he had lost her.

The silence around him deepened.

He continued toward the bedroom - alone. The phone rang just as Mark was locking away the day's files. He checked the screen.

Meena.

He answered.

'Meena, it's late. Everything alright?'

'Relax, Dr Mark,' her voice came, brisk and familiar. 'Just calling to check if tomorrow's press conference is going to feature the real Mark - the rationalist people worship or the diplomatic one police prefer.'

'I didn't know I had two versions.'

'Everyone does,' she said. 'Especially you. And yes, before you say it -' there was a teasing edge in her tone, 'I do admire your work. Your clarity. Your scientific approach. Your spine. But…'

He waited.

'But you refuse to join us,' she finished. 'You'd be an asset to our organisation. A voice like yours could change this state. You know that.'

Mark slanted against the wall, looking out at the dimly lit courtyard.

'I've told you before, Meena. I value your movement. But your organisation fights all traditions - even the harmless ones. Even the ones that hold communities together. Culture isn't the enemy.'

'Culture becomes the enemy when it chains people,' she countered quietly. 'You know that better than anyone.'

'And sometimes,' Mark replied with restraint, 'culture is

the rope that keeps society from falling apart.'

There was a soft exhale on the other end.

'You're impossible, Mark.'

'So are you.'

'Anyway,' she said finally, her tone lighter, 'don't slip up tomorrow. People listen when you speak. Even those who don't want to.'

'I won't,' he promised.

'Good. And Mark?'

'Yes?'

'Just because you don't join us... doesn't mean I've stopped admiring you.'

He felt warmth flicker beneath the exhaustion.

'I know.'

The call ended, leaving the night quiet again.

There was an unusual crowd at the press conference. This wasn't the usual neat line of journalists with notepads and microphones. The crowd had swelled into a chaotic mix of reporters elbowing for space, politicians lingering in corners with tight faces, activists whispering urgently among themselves and clusters of wide-eyed, superstitious onlookers who had come hoping to witness an exorcism disguised as a press briefing.

Cameras flashed like lightning across the room. The hum of anxious chatter rose and fell like a tide.

On the dais, Mark took his seat beside Commissioner Vikram and the senior investigation officers. The long desk before them was cluttered with microphones - glossy, colourful, branded logos of every news channel in Kerala, plus newer online platforms and amateur livestreamers hungry for sensational footage.

Mark adjusted the collar of his shirt, exhaled slowly and looked at the sea of expectant eyes.

Commissioner Vikram tipped forward and cleared his throat.

'The unnatural death of MLA Anwar has been cracked by the Kerala Police,' he announced. 'This was made possible with the help of our official consultant, Dr Markandeyan. He will explain the rest.'

Dozens of cameras turned toward Mark with a near-predatory snap.

He leaned toward the microphone.

'Hello, everyone,' he began, calm and steady. 'We conducted a thorough examination of the body, the vehicle and all associated evidence. What happened to MLA Anwar may have appeared supernatural to the public, but the truth is far more human and far more dangerous.'

The cameras zoomed in.

'The victim entered his car. This vehicle was a recent model - a smart car, fully software-controlled. A hacker remotely accessed the system and locked the doors, preventing the driver or anyone else from opening them. An electrical pulse triggered from the same system ensured no one could force their way in.'

Murmurs rippled through the crowd.

'The hacker then activated the AC ducts, releasing a gas intended to weaken and disorient the victim. Immediately after, the airbags were deployed by the same hacker. But these airbags had been tampered with. They contained concentrated methanol. The methanol coated the victim's skin,' Mark continued, voice even but clipped. 'Finally, the hacker initiated a spark inside the car by shorting the wiring circuit. Anwar managed to escape through a broken window… but the methanol had already soaked into him.'

He paused, letting the weight of the moment settle.

'Methanol burns with an invisible flame in bright daylight.

That is why no one saw fire. That is why the crowd believed something supernatural was happening. But it was a chemical burn. Intense, fast and tragically unseen.'

'Invisible? Can you explain methanol fire?' a reporter raised a hand.

'Yes,' Mark said. 'Usually, fire becomes visible because the burning substance releases luminous particles like tiny glowing bits of soot. In normal flames, especially from petrol, wood or candle, these particles glow yellow or orange, which the eye can easily see. But methanol burns clean. Almost no soot. Almost no glowing particles. The flame it produces is very pale, almost bluish. And when you place that pale-blue flame in bright sunlight, the light from the sun completely washes it out. Your eyes cannot detect it. Go outside on a bright day and light a gas stove. Even the blue flame becomes nearly invisible. Methanol is far worse. The flames vanish into the sunlight. That is what happened.'

'So the fire was really there, but no one could see it?'

'Exactly,' Mark said. 'The fire was burning him every second. But to the crowd, it looked as if his skin was blistering for no reason. They assumed something paranormal because they couldn't see the cause. The fire became visible only when the methanol ignited his clothes, as the cotton and polyester began to burn, producing yellow-orange flames and black soot. But by then, people had already accepted the paranormal narrative.'

He paused, then added, 'If the incident had happened at dusk or indoors, the flames would've been bright, blue and unmistakable. But under a tropical sun, methanol fire becomes practically invisible. That's why the onlookers had no idea what was happening. If the people around him hadn't frozen in fear, believing they were witnessing a curse. Anwar could have been saved. But superstition paralysed them. No one dared to step forward.'

'Where was the methanol stored?' another reporter shot up.

Mark gestured toward the forensic team.

'Inside the vehicle we found additional canisters and holders installed illegally. According to Anwar's driver, the car was purchased recently from an unauthorized seller. The car company refused responsibility…stating the car had been tampered with before Anwar bought it by the unauthorized seller.'

The room erupted with muttering, pens scratching furiously.

'Who was the seller?' a journalist demanded.

Mark hesitated just a second, but enough.

Commissioner Vikram stepped in smoothly.

'Dr Markandeyan's job was to establish the cause of death,' he said. 'Identifying the suspect is our duty. According to the driver, only MLA Anwar knew the seller's identity. We are investigating and will apprehend the culprit soon.'

Reporters surged forward with louder questions now. One man stood up.

'Dr Markandeyan,' he called out, 'please comment on the widespread belief that this was a curse or supernatural punishment.'

A hush fell.

Mark dipped forward, eyes hardening.

'The only curse affecting this society is superstition,' he said. His voice was sharp enough to slice through the static of cameras. 'People should fear criminals - not ghosts. Demons do not kill. Humans do. I want to emphasize this clearly.'

He paused.

'There are no curses.'

Every news channel repeated it instantly.

Every social media feed lit up.

And somewhere in the city, in a cramped house filled with fear, someone froze at that sentence.

'There are no curses.'

Someone who believed they were living under a real curse.

Someone desperate.

Someone who would soon seek out Dr Mark about a cursed salt said to have damned an entire colony.

CHAPTER TWO

The Ghost of 5E

Kavya found herself far from the misty hills of Idukki. At twenty seven, after years of coaching centres, late night revisions and writing Public Service Commission exams until her fingers grew numb, she had finally claimed the victory her family prayed for. A government job in Thiruvananthapuram. The Secretariat itself.

Through the internet, she found a small apartment close enough to walk to the Secretariat. The rent was high, far beyond what she had hoped for, but it was the cheapest available in the busy heart of the capital. The building was old, probably built before her parents were born, its paint stained and its staircases chipped by time.

She climbed six floors every day to reach her apartment marked 5E. By the time she reached the landing, her breath would be shallow and sweat clung to her temples. The corridor smelled faintly of dampness. The moment she opened her door, the humidity wrapped her like a wet blanket.

The apartment had a hall, a tiny kitchen, a narrow

bathroom and a single bedroom. Fresh paint on the walls did little to hide how old everything truly was. The cupboard creaked whenever she opened it. The electrical switches felt brittle. The tap in the kitchen sputtered before releasing water. When she opened the bedroom window, the roar of the city rushed inside at once, carrying the smell of exhaust fumes, dust and something metallic. She quickly shut it, locking the world out again.

Whenever she opened her main door for ventilation, the young bachelors living in other rooms would peek in while passing. She caught their eyes once, then immediately closed the door and pulled the latch. The air turned warmer, heavier, but she preferred the suffocation to the unwanted attention. Leaving was not an option either. She had paid the deposit and the eleven month clause stated the owner need not return it if she left earlier. She sighed and told herself she would endure it. After eleven months she would buy a scooter and shift somewhere quieter, even if it meant living far from the Secretariat. Peace was worth the distance.

Her days settled into a simple and mechanical rhythm. She woke at seven each morning. On her electric stove she prepared idly or dosa, sometimes just bread and tea if she felt too tired. She had lunch at the Secretariat canteen. Dinner was either chapatis she made at night or parcels she bought on her way back. Before sleeping, she curled up on her bed and watched films on her laptop. The glow of the screen was the only comforting light in the cramped room.

Each morning she walked down six floors. She crossed the basement parking area which felt like the inside of a rusted tin box. Only a metal gate allowed light in. She stepped outside into the busy city and walked to work.

The first week wore her out more than she expected. Her eyes were dull, her voice sounded flat and she found it hard to stay cheerful.

One afternoon, her co-worker Usha, a warm woman in her forties with a kind round face, approached her with concern.

'Why do you seem always tired?' Usha asked politely, placing a stack of files on her desk.

Kavya rubbed her forehead. 'I was eating well and sleeping well back in my village. The capital city feels too much. The pollution, the heat, the noise, even the food tastes different. My body is not taking it calmly.'

'Don't worry. It will take time to adjust. And like all the others who come to Thiruvananthapuram for work, one day you will buy a house here and settle after retirement,' Usha laughed softly.

'That is highly unlikely.' Kavya chuckled.

Usha shook her head with amusement and walked away.

Kavya hoped that things would improve in the coming days. But, on the third morning, she woke with heaviness. Her head throbbed dully. Her eyes burned. She blamed the heat and the sixth–floor climb. She dragged herself out of bed and stared at her reflection. Her skin looked pale, almost greyish under the shaky bathroom tube-light.

'Maybe I just need rest,' she murmured.

But rest did not help. Nothing did.

That evening, while boiling milk, she caught something move near the kitchen doorway. It was quick. A black flicker, almost like a moth's shadow. She turned sharply, eyes narrowed.

Nothing.

Just the empty doorway and the dim corridor.

She frowned, annoyed with herself and resumed her tea.

Another flicker. This time near the floor, like a shadow sliding along the tiles. She spun, her hair whipping over her shoulder.

The room stood still, silent.

She tried to laugh it off, but her smile trembled. Her hands felt strangely cold. She wrapped her arms around herself and went to bed early.

By Day Four, she stopped pretending nothing was wrong.

Shadows danced at the edges of her sight constantly now. While folding clothes, she would see a dark blur crouching near the cupboard. When she worked on her laptop in the hall, a shadow would glide across the opposite wall. Whenever she turned her head directly, the shape dissolved like smoke.

It was evening when she heard the first soft knock. Three faint taps. She froze. It came again. Not from the door, but from inside the walls.

Then came a sound like cloth rustling. Her breath stopped halfway in her throat. The rustling moved… across the bedroom. Then stopped.

She tiptoed to the door and peeked outside. The corridor remained empty, though she thought she heard a soft sigh coming from it. Or maybe it was the wind. Or maybe-

Footsteps.

Slow. Dragging. From the far end of the corridor.

She shut the door immediately, bolting it with shaking hands.

She curled on her bed that night, hugging a pillow, shivering. Every little vibration of the building felt magnified, like someone breathing against her ear.

She woke up the next day, exhausted like usual.

She yelled at a cup for slipping from her hand. She burst into tears when she couldn't find her other garment. She laughed hysterically for two minutes straight when her dosa burnt up. Then she stared at the torn piece on the pan and felt a strange creeping dread.

The room felt heavier, like the air itself had thickened. Her head spun every time she bent down. The lights flickered more than usual. Even her shadow on the wall looked… darker.

She was dizzy and dull during work. She had dinner at a restaurant, being too tired to cook at home.

After reaching her room she felt icy cold. Goosebumps crawled across her arms. Five minutes later the heat punched her like a furnace. Sweat trickled down her neck. The temperature danced unpredictably, like some invisible force stroking her skin with cold fingers, then suddenly pressing burning palms against her shoulders.

As she lay on the narrow bed, staring at the ceiling fan that groaned with every slow rotation, a thought flickered through Kavya's mind. Perhaps she should tell someone. Usha. A friend from home. Anyone. Someone who could listen without the shadows twisting the meaning of her words.

But then she imagined their reactions. The laughter masked as concern. The raised eyebrows. The whispered comments behind her back. Small-town girl goes to the city and loses her mind. The humiliation made her stomach tighten. She pulled the blanket up to her chin and turned to the wall, forcing her eyes shut.

No. She would keep this to herself.

The next morning, still groggy from another night of broken sleep, Kavya shuffled to the bathroom with her toothbrush in hand. As she walked back across the tiny room, something caught her eye. The pack of post-it notes she had bought weeks ago, still sealed in its plastic last night, now sat open on the table. The wrapper lay torn beside it.

That wasn't all.

A single post-it note lay on the floor near the foot of her bed, its neon edge bright against the dull tiles. It looked as though someone had dropped it while standing right where she slept.

She picked it up.

The note said, in a hurried scrawl:

YOU FORGOT TO LOCK THE DOOR LAST NIGHT. BE CAREFUL.

She read it twice. The handwriting wasn't hers. Jagged, uneven, written by a trembling hand. The message made her chest tighten. She tried to recall the previous night. She saw only fragments. Her own face swimming in darkness. A choking smell in the room. A shadow leaning over her bed.

She tore the note down and threw it into the dustbin.

The next morning, another note waited on the kitchen counter.

YOU LEFT THE LIGHTS ON. CHECK IT AGAIN.

She hid the note inside a drawer and tried not to think about it.

By nightfall she felt watched again. Her skin prickled. Her breath came shallow and hot. Something was whispering inside the walls. She could hear it when she stood still. Kavya switched on every light and sat on the bed. She tried to keep her eyes open but exhaustion finally dragged her down. She slept sitting up, head tilted, mouth open.

When she woke, three more post-it notes were stuck to the cupboard door.

PLEASE TAKE CARE OF YOURSELF.

YOU ARE NOT SAFE WHEN YOU SLEEP.

HE IS STANDING BEHIND YOU.

She screamed and flung herself away from the door. Her back hit the wall. Her breath came in gasps. She looked around the room with wide eyes. The lights were on. The curtains still. Nothing moved.

Yet she could not shake the feeling that someone had just

stepped out of sight. Perhaps into the bathroom. Perhaps behind the bedroom door. Perhaps crouched beneath her bed.

She crept to the cupboard, ripped the notes down.

The next night, sleep came to Kavya like a thief. She slid into it, heavy and breathless and the dreams drowned her whole. Events unfolded later. She woke fully conscious but unable to move. Her breath halted halfway. Her chest felt crushed under a hundred invisible hands.

There was someone in the room.

She could hear them. She could feel them.

A slight dip on the edge of her bed. A weight. A slow shift of the mattress.

Her eyes darted wildly but her body refused to obey. She wanted to scream. Her throat made only a thin whimpering sound. She felt as though someone was sitting on top of her and pinning her arms to the bed that she couldn't move.

Kavya knew there is nothing she could do. So she closed her eyes and let it be. As she drifted toward sleep she saw a face forming in the darkness above her. First an outline, then hollow eyes, then the faint suggestion of a mouth that stretched and curved as if speaking her name.

She woke up the next day with clear exhaustion.

She jerked awake, sweating.

The next night, the doorframe bent slightly as if the entire room was tilting. A silhouette inclined inside, long and angular.

She blinked once. Twice.

The silhouette remained.

Then slowly dissolved.

She no longer trusted her own eyes.

Her hands shook constantly. She could not sleep without lights, yet when the lights were on, shadows moved anyway.

More and more post-it notes, most of them blanks most of them have unintelligible messages appeared all over the rooms. Sometimes under the bed, sometimes under her books.

Almost two weeks has passed. Kavya had just returned from work and was reaching for the fridge when she froze. A tall dark shape stood beside it. Taller than any human she had ever seen. Shoulders too broad. Head tilted like a curious dog that is about to bite.

The shape did not move.

Neither did she.

Then it slid silently behind the bathroom door and melted into the darkness.

She backed away until her spine pressed against the wall. The feeling of being watched pressed into her skin like cold needles.

When she was in the bathroom, the tiles swirled with moisture patterns. Except now they were not patterns. They were faces. Dozens of them. Glaring. Twisted. Their mouths curled downward in hatred.

She pressed both hands against her ears and squeezed her eyes shut.

Kavya was convinced that someone was inside the flat. She could feel the presence constantly. It pressed against her back when she walked. It stood behind the bathroom door when she showered. It crouched in the hall while she cooked.

She left all the lights on. She slept with the videos playing at full volume. Still the room felt crowded with invisible bodies that breathed just behind her.

Kavya spent the next evening curled on the narrow bed. The room lit only by the weak tube light buzzing overhead. She wanted answers. She wanted a solution. Something was wrong in that flat and she could no longer pretend it was stress or imagination. With trembling fingers she opened YouTube and typed keywords she had never typed in her life: haunted apartment, ghost in house, how to remove ghost Kerala.

Dozens of videos appeared. Some ridiculous. Some unsettling. One thumbnail stopped her. A moustacheless-orange-bearded man in white kurta, staring straight into the camera with reddened eyes. His name was written boldly below.

Rashid Parambilmana.

The comments praised him. Hundreds of viewers claiming he solved their hauntings. Stills of his "investigations" flashed in thumbnails. Interviews where he described Jinns, night demons, curses placed on houses.

Kavya clicked one. His voice, rasping and harsh like a toad being scraped across rough stone, filled the room.

'Jinns manifest where the air is stale,' he said, pointing at a dark corridor behind him. 'First they whisper. Then they feed on fear. Then they take form.'

She watched another. And another. Hours passed. She did not notice the time. She did not notice the temperature in the room rising and falling. She only felt that something in Rashid's words fit her situation too closely.

A number flashed at the bottom of the screen.

Her heart was thundering. Her hands were cold. Still, she dialled.

The call connected.

'Hello,' came the rasp she recognised.

She hesitated. 'Is this Rashid Parambilmana sir…?'

'Yes. Tell me.'

'I think… I think my apartment is haunted.'

There was a short pause. Then a flat instruction. 'Send a picture of the apartment in WhatsApp.'

She took a shaky photograph of the hall, uploaded it and waited. A new image arrived seconds later. A QR code.

Below it, the note read: Online Consulting Fee ₹3000.

She stared. Then exhaled. She had no one else to turn to.

Her fear was stronger than her hesitance. She opened her UPI app and paid.

The next message from him surprised her.

Send your selfie. Only then I can make consultation.

If he had asked this in the beginning she would have blocked him instantly. But now she had paid three thousand rupees. She could not lose it. She took a picture, avoiding her own frightened eyes and sent it.

The phone rang again.

'Tell me what is your problem,' Rashid said.

She explained everything. The shadows. The dreams. The notes. The voices. The suffocating feeling inside the house.

Rashid breathed heavily into the mic. 'This is a clear case of a ghost feeding on energy. It begins with discomfort. Then it adjusts to your chemistry. Then it grows stronger by drinking your fear. Now it is manifesting. If you delay action, it will attack in a week.'

'Will it kill me?' her voice broke.

'That is the safest possibility,' Rashid replied without emotion. 'It may push you down the stairs. It may strangle you while you sleep. Worst of all, it may possess your body and live as you. You will remain dead inside.'

A panic rose in her chest like something alive. She began to cry.

'Do not cry, child,' rasped Rashid. 'I have handled many such cases successfully.'

'What if I leave the apartment?' she whispered.

'No use,' he said. 'It has tasted your scent. It will follow you wherever you go. You must fight it now.'

'What should I do?' she whimpered.

'I will come to perform a sacrifice,' said Rashid. 'For the ritual, the holy items and my service, the cost is one lakh rupees.'

She sobbed louder. 'I do not have that much money… I only just got this job. My parents are farmers. They cannot help.'

'It is a matter of life and death. Money will come and go. Think about it,' he said and the line clicked off.

Her breath quivered. She looked toward the wall and froze. Another face. Another twisted shadow forming in the cracks of the paint. She bolted out of the flat, stumbling down the six flights of stairs until she reached the open air. It was already past eleven. She sat on a bench in the nearby park, shaking, hugging herself, thinking of how she could gather a lakh. Thinking of the darkness in her room waiting for her.

She walked back only when the fear of the night outside grew stronger than the fear inside.

Her phone rang again.

Rashid.

She answered cautiously.

'I felt bad for you,' he said, his voice softer. 'So I made some calls. There is one last option, but it is something I never offer lightly. My assistant in Thiruvananthapuram has an item. Not an ordinary charm. This is the final piece he brought from Yemen. It is centuries old, carved and blessed in the old Arabian way, the kind that was used even before written history. Very rare. There are people who would pay lakhs for it, but it is not for sale. Not at any price.'

He paused, as if weighing something sacred.

'My assistant had saved it for a very serious case, but after hearing your situation, and only because I instructed him, he agreed to use it for you. He has only this one. It repels even the strongest Jinns. But… you need to pay him fifteen thousand rupees for the ritual work. He will come tomorrow and apply it in your room.'

Relief exploded inside her. Fifteen thousand she could

manage. Barely. It would mean cutting meals and skipping bills. But her life mattered more.

'I agree,' she said breathlessly.

'I will send him your number,' said Rashid. 'He will contact you. The cleansing must be done tomorrow.'

'But sir, I have office tomorrow,' she whispered.

'Take leave. Your life is priority number one.'

Kavya answered softly, even though he could not see her. 'Yes… yes, sir.'

She hung up and looked up at the night sky. For the first time in weeks, she felt a flicker of hope.

Kavya took leave from work the next morning. She spent the early hours pacing her tiny flat, palms sweating, checking the clock again and again. At ten, the sound of a motorcycle echoed through the narrow street below. She heard the door bell within a few minutes. She opened the door to see the man in black kurta, a cloth bag slung over his shoulder.

'Abdulla?' she asked, opening the door a crack.

'Yes,' he replied, stepping inside with assured confidence. His eyes wandered across the cramped hall and the closed bedroom door. He inhaled deeply, then frowned.

'I can feel the negative energy in here,' he said, lowering his voice. 'It is heavy. Thick. Someone must have conjured it with black magic. Perhaps a previous tenant left their stain behind.'

A cold tremor ran down Kavya's spine.

'Do not fear,' Abdulla said, placing the bag on the floor. 'With this charm from Arabia, no ghost or jinn will dare approach you again.'

'Please,' whispered Kavya. 'Please do whatever is needed.'

Abdulla pulled out a small bottle filled with a cloudy liquid.

'This,' he said with reverence, 'is water from a divine well in Arabia. People travel across deserts for a single drop.'

He dipped his fingers into the bottle and flicked the liquid around the hall, the bedroom, even the bathroom, muttering soft Arabic syllables between each gesture.

Next, he placed a wide clay bowl on the floor and filled it with charcoal, coconut husk and coarse dark fragments whose smell made her step back. He struck a match; flames rose slowly, eating through the husk. Smoke curled upward, heavy and damp.

Then he reached into the bag again and produced a small opaque bottle, holding it as though it were fragile as an eggshell.

'This,' he said, 'is the mystic substance from Yemen. Very old. Very rare. Only one such bottle remains in our hands.'

He uncorked it, murmured Arabic chants and emptied the powder into the fire. Instantly the smoke thickened, swirling with an unsettling sweetness that clung to the skin.

'It is done,' Abdulla said, brushing his hands and standing up. 'You must leave now. The smoke will fill every corner. In these hours there will be a battle between the divine and the evil spirit. You must not stay inside. There can be casualties.'

'Casualties?' she asked, terrified.

'Yes. Better not interfere.' He stepped to the door. 'Come.'

She followed him out to the corridor. The door closed behind them with a soft thud.

'Did Rashid ikka tell you about the payment?' he asked casually.

'Yes… I will send it now,' she said, unlocking her phone with trembling fingers.

She transferred the money. Abdulla checked his screen, nodded once and walked down the stairs without looking back.

Left alone in the corridor, Kavya clutched her handbag and exhaled shakily. She spent the rest of the day trying to distract herself. She went to a movie, ate lunch in a small restaurant, wandered the city. Each minute felt like a stone pressing on her chest.

By evening she returned to the apartment with renewed hope. She pushed open the door. The flat was hazy with perfumed smoke. Something about the air felt different, calmer.

She allowed herself a smile.

She showered, had a light dinner and soon felt overwhelmingly sleepy. She collapsed into bed and slept deeply for the first time in days.

In the morning, she woke dizzy. The bathroom spun around her. She leaned on the wall, steadying herself. A faint sense of dread still clung to her. She tried to ignore it.

She decided to buy breakfast outside. Anything to leave the suffocating room behind.

But as she stepped into the corridor, a chill crept along her spine. She felt watched. Followed.

She hurried down the stairs. Behind her, something seemed to move, just a whisper of presence, just enough to make her heart pound. She gripped the railing and quickened her pace.

Halfway down, the unseen pressure intensified. She felt breath on her neck. A push. A firm, unmistakable shove.

The world flipped. The staircase blurred.

Then darkness closed over her.

She woke to bright lights and antiseptic smell, lying on a hospital bed, head throbbing, surrounded by the steady beep of machines.

It looked like the Emergency ward. Harsh white lights hummed overhead and the smell of antiseptic lingered like a film on the air. Kavya blinked slowly, her vision settling on a nurse hurrying past with a tray of syringes.

'Hello… sister,' she whispered, her throat dry. 'Where am I? Who brought me here?'

The nurse paused, glanced at her chart, then at Kavya's face.

'You are in TOS Hospital,' she said gently. 'You had a fall and hit your head. Nothing too serious, just a short loss of consciousness. Your friend has gone to pay the bills.' She adjusted the IV line. 'How are you feeling now?'

'I have a headache,' murmured Kavya.

'The IV drip contains painkillers. The doctor will check on you soon.' And with that, the nurse moved on.

Friend?

What friend?

Before she could make sense of it, a young man and woman stepped into the cubicle. Both appeared to be in their late twenties.

'How are you feeling?' the man asked, leaning forward.

'I… I don't know. Who are you?' she asked, genuinely confused.

'Great. She doesn't even recognise the guy who saved her life,' the woman muttered.

'It's alright, Jyolsna,' said the man. 'We've never properly met.'

'I'm sorry,' Kavya said, struggling to sit up. 'I've never seen you.'

'I'm your neighbour. Same building,' he said with an awkward smile. 'I'm Rakesh. I work in a news portal. Jyolsna is a journalist there, my colleague. I was on my way to office when I found you unconscious on the steps. I brought you here. I called Jyolsna for help.'

Kavya's eyes widened.

'Did you… see the ghost?'

'Ghost?' Rakesh and Jyolsna echoed, staring at her.

She realised immediately how strange she must sound.

'I mean… I just… forget it.'

'What happened?' asked Jyolsna, pulling a chair closer.

'No, it's nothing,' said Kavya, shrinking back into the pillow.

'You can tell me,' said Jyolsna softly. 'I might be able to help.'

Kavya hesitated.

Jyolsna turned to Rakesh.

'Rakesh, go to office and mark my leave. I'll stay with her today.'

Rakesh nodded and left the cubicle.

Once he was gone, Jyolsna spoke again.

'Now that the guy has left, maybe you can tell me if it is something… sensitive. Something you'd prefer only another woman to hear.'

'No. Nothing like that,' said Kavya, embarrassed. 'It's just… you won't believe me.'

'Try me. Or wait, I'll bring breakfast. You rest and we'll talk.'

She left. Kavya lay there thinking, her heart fluttering with the weight of everything she had kept to herself. Maybe she needed to tell someone. Maybe she had no other choice.

Jyolsna returned with a packet of idlis and chutney.

'Okay,' she said, pulling up the chair again, 'now talk. I will feed you in between.'

Kavya took a deep breath and narrated everything. Every hallucination, every shadow, every whisper, every terrifying night. The ritual. The smoke. Abdulla. Rashid.

When she finished, Jyolsna looked thoughtful, not shocked.

'Right,' she said, wiping her hands. 'You need a professional ghost hunter for this.'

'So you believe me?' asked Kavya, eyes wide and trembling. 'But Rashid Parambilmana is a professional ghost hunter. Even he could not fix this.'

'No, no,' said Jyolsna, shaking her head. 'Those people use old methods. Rites and drama. Nowadays, there are modern instruments. Devices that detect paranormal signatures and machines that could trap evil entities. Haven't you seen Ghostbusters?'

'Modern ghost hunters?' Kavya whispered miserably. 'I do not have money for that kind of people. I might as well die.'

'Hey, hey, do not cry,' said Jyolsna, touching her shoulder. 'I know someone. Personally. He will help you for free. He owes me a favour.'

'Really?' whispered Kavya, hope flickering inside her for the first time in days. 'What is his name?'

Jyolsna smiled.

'Dr Mark.'

CHAPTER THREE
Invisible Demon

Kavya returned to her small government quarters that evening, her head still aching faintly from the fall. Usha from the Secretariat accompanied her, carrying a bag of fruits and talking in her usual calm, motherly tone. Jyolsna was with her as well. She watched Kavya closely for any sign of distress.

Kavya and Jyolsna silently agreed that Usha did not need to hear a single word about ghosts, rituals or hallucinations.

'You look tired, child,' Usha said, placing the fruits on the table. 'Try to rest well.'

After Usha left, closing the door behind her, Jyolsna turned to Kavya.

'Dr Mark will come on Sunday,' she said. 'He is free only then. I will also be here. Until that day, you must not stay alone in this room. Come to my house for a few days.'

Kavya hesitated.

'But Rashid said the ghost is attached to me,' she whispered. 'He said it will follow me wherever I go. What if it comes to your house? What if it hurts someone there?'

Jyolsna snorted lightly, waving a hand dismissively.

'You do not have to worry about that,' she said. 'My house is equipped with many ghost and demon repelling technologies. Ghosts are scared to enter. Trust me, you will be safe.'

'Are you sure?' asked Kavya, searching her face.

'Trust me, girl,' replied Jyolsna with a reassuring smile. 'Nothing supernatural can come near my house.'

Kavya bowed her head slightly, wanting to believe her.

The next three days passed inside Jyolsna's home, a neat two-storey house where her parents lived. It was warm, cluttered with books and old framed photos and always filled with the comforting sounds of someone cooking or someone talking. Every morning, Jyolsna would drop Kavya at the Secretariat on her scooter before heading to her newsroom.

To Kavya's surprise, the nights passed without incident. No cold spots. No moving shadows. No whispering voices. No suffocating dread sitting on her chest. She slept deeply for the first time in weeks.

One evening after dinner, curiosity finally pushed her to ask.

'Can I see all those machines in your house?' asked Kavya shyly. 'The ones that repel evil?'

'Oh, those,' she said quickly. 'They are fitted inside the foundation. Below the basement. Some inside the walls. They are not visible like normal gadgets. Do not worry, you will understand everything when Dr Mark explains the physics and chemistry behind them.'

Kavya accepted this explanation with a relieved sigh. And so she waited with hope and fear woven tightly through her thoughts. She counted the hours, the minutes, wanting Sunday to arrive faster.

At last, the day came. The Sunday when Dr Mark would

finally step into her nightmare. The morning light felt different. Heavy. Anticipating.

Jyolsna stayed close to Kavya inside the apartment, her presence steady like an anchor. She was the one who had contacted Dr Mark, arranged everything and now waited with folded arms and restless eyes.

The doorbell rang.

Kavya felt her breath catch. Jyolsna hurried to the door and opened it. Two men stood outside in the corridor. One looked composed, eyes sharp behind square spectacles. The other carried a briefcase.

'So, you are Kavya?' Mark asked. His voice was calm.

'Yes,' she replied, trying to steady her voice.

'Alright. Let us hunt some ghosts.'

Mark stepped inside with theatrical ceremony. Kavya watched as he stretched out both hands, palms facing the air. He closed his eyes and inhaled deeply, as if tasting the atmosphere of the room. Then he coughed harshly, bending slightly forward.

'Oh… right,' he said, rubbing his throat. 'There is a heavy build up of negative energy here. I can feel it thick in the air.'

Kavya shivered. Her fingers dug into the ends of her shawl.

Dr Mark turned to his companion.

'Ashok, give me the detector.'

Ashok opened the case and took out a device that looked strangely like an oversized AC remote. It was yellow and black, with a glass bulb at the top and a small LCD screen. Mark took it, pressed a button and the screen flickered to life with a faint green glow.

Kavya watched with wide eyes. The device emitted rapid, violent beeping that echoed off the walls. Numbers flashed and jumped wildly across the screen.

'It is worse than I expected,' said Mark, his brows drawing together.

He walked slowly through the apartment, holding the device forward like a compass. He scanned the corners, the ceiling, the gaps between furniture, even the crack near the bathroom door. The beeping intensified.

'It has its presence everywhere,' he murmured.

Kavya felt tears sting her eyes. Her body trembled from the cold fear pressing against her ribs. Mark looked at her. His face softened but the seriousness in his tone remained.

'You are very fortunate that you are still alive. The situation here is far more dangerous than you realise.'

'Can you contain it and take it away?' Kavya asked in desperation.

'There is no need to bind the ghost,' he replied.

He walked swiftly to the windows and pushed them open one by one. Harsh sunlight spilled into the room with the city's dust.

'Most spirits disperse when the windows are opened. They cannot stay in moving air.'

'What?' Kavya stared at him. 'That is it? Won't it come back?'

'This one has already gone,' said Mark. 'But that is not the true problem. We must understand where the ghosts are coming from in the first place.'

He studied the room again. He moved through the kitchen, checking the walls and ceiling and then stepped into the bathroom, tracing the outlines of pipes and vents with careful eyes. It looked less like a ritual and more like an investigation.

'Come. Follow me,' he said at last.

Mark and Ashok stepped out of the apartment. Kavya glanced at Jyolsna, who gestured for her to come along. They walked down the stairs to the basement parking. The air smelled of oil and smoke.

Mark moved purposefully across the concrete floor, examining the structure above. He stopped near a square opening in the ceiling where the roofing was missing. The opening stretched all the way up the building like a hollow shaft.

A small generator sat directly beneath it, paint peeling, vibrating slightly as if it had been recently used.

'Yes,' said Mark quietly. 'The ghosts originate here.'

'Was someone killed here?' she asked. Kavya's heart pounded.

'No,' Mark replied. 'The troublemaker is created here daily.'

Kavya stared at him. The words made no sense. Her confusion twisted into fear.

Jyolsna chuckled under her breath.

'I do not understand,' said Kavya, voice shaking. 'Somebody please tell me what is happening.'

'The evil entity haunting you, young lady, is not a ghost or a demon or a jinn,' said Mark, his voice lowering as if he were unveiling the final twist of a stage performance. His eyes gleamed behind his glasses. 'It is just an invisible gas called carbon monoxide.'

For a moment, Kavya simply stared at him. She was visibly confused.

Mark turned slowly in the basement with his boots scraping against the dusty concrete. Shadows from the stacked scooters and parked cars stretched long and crooked under the dim tube lights.

'We are in the basement where everyone parks their vehicles,' he continued. 'Every day, someone starts a scooter or car here and lets it idle. Exhaust fumes build up and drift into this shaft. And look there.'

He pointed at the small, battered generator, half hidden behind a concrete pillar. It sat humming like something alive, its casing stained with soot.

'They run this old petrol generator too. All of this releases fumes. You know what is in that smoke? Carbon monoxide. It drifts up through this ventilation structure.' He pointed at the hollow chamber above them, a square well of blackness rising through the seven storeys.

Kavya followed his gaze. The shaft looked like a throat leading into darkness.

'The smoke is supposed to go up,' Mark said. 'But your symptoms tell me it is not escaping properly. I suspect the top is blocked. Come. Let us check.'

The walk up seven floors felt endless. The stairwell was poorly lit and their footsteps echoed like distant knocks. Kavya could feel her pulse thudding in her throat.

At the rooftop, harsh sunlight flooded the space. The wind whipped lightly around them. Mark approached the square structure that rose from the roof like a chimney. Its mouth was covered with a sheet of asbestos.

'There it is,' he said. 'Completely sealed.'

'Why would they close it?' asked Ashok, wiping sweat from his forehead.

Mark crouched near the sheet, tracing its edges with his fingers. 'This building is old,' he said. 'When it was built, the designers never imagined dozens of vehicles running in the basement every morning. This shaft was probably meant only for tiny bathroom ventilation slits.' He tapped the sheet. 'This covering looks like a later addition. Perhaps after heavy rains, they decided to prevent water from entering the shaft. But by closing it, they trapped all the fumes inside.'

Kavya felt her stomach twist. She looked down the shaft

again. It felt as though something cold reached up from it.

'But why does only Kavya suffer? Why not the other tenants?' Jyolsna crossed her arms.

Mark stood and looked at her. 'Because others open their windows. Even a small draft helps blow the carbon monoxide out. But Kavya.' He turned to her. 'You keep everything shut. Doors. Windows. Curtains. You trap the gas inside with you.'

Kavya pressed a hand to her mouth.

'But what does this carbon monoxide has to do with the hauntings?' asked Kavya.

'Come, let's go to your room and I'll explain it to you,' said Mark.

'Thanks. Couldn't bear the heat here,' said Ashok.

As they reached the room, Mark started -

'Carbon monoxide is formed whenever something burns without enough oxygen. Vehicles, especially old ones, do that all the time. When a scooter or car is idling in a closed space like this, the engine burns fuel, but the air around it is limited. The combustion is incomplete. Instead of producing harmless carbon dioxide, it creates carbon monoxide.'

'Incomplete combustion,' Ashok added quietly. 'That is the key.'

Mark nodded. 'Exactly. Imagine fire gasping for air. It cannot breathe properly. So it produces poison instead of normal smoke. The fumes rise like warm breath. Every morning and evening when people start their scooters, clouds of exhaust drift up through the ventilation structure like a chimney. It is supposed to escape out of the top. But because the top is sealed, the gas simply collects and flows into the nearest openings. In this case, the bathroom vents of your floor.'

He pointed to her bathroom vent as though the ghost itself were lurking behind it.

'And carbon monoxide is tricky,' Mark said. 'You cannot see it. You cannot smell it. Your body does not recognise it as danger. It quietly replaces oxygen in your blood and your brain starts to starve.'

Kavya drew a tight breath. 'So every time someone starts a bike down here, the gas goes up and… enters my flat.'

'Yes,' Mark said.

'But…but…you haven't still explained how it is connected to the ghosts,' said Kavya.

'Let's all go to my home and have lunch there,' said Mark. 'I'll explain everything there.'

Kavya and Jyolsna agreed.

Mark opened the front door, the corridor inside dim and cool. There were books everywhere, stacked in even piles, shelves packed with medical journals, psychology texts, radiation manuals, forensic binders and old chemistry models. The air smelled faintly of camphor and old paper.

'Come in,' said Mark, gesturing them forward. 'I wanted to bring you here because you need to see something properly. An explanation inside your apartment would not have been enough.'

Kavya stepped in hesitantly. She expected incense, talismans, something spiritual. Instead, she found a small room that looked almost like a science classroom. There was a whiteboard, small models of atoms, a dismantled smoke detector, a few test tubes and a large box marked GAS ANALYSER.

'Sit here,' said Mark, pulling out chairs. 'I want you to understand exactly what haunted you.'

He picked up the same yellow and black device he had used earlier.

'This is where we start,' he said. 'This detector first told me the real story. I used it in your room and it showed dangerously high levels of carbon monoxide.'

He set it on the table. It beeped softly.

'Now listen to me carefully,' said Mark, rubbing his hands together as if preparing for a lecture. 'What I am about to explain is the science behind every shadow you saw, every whisper you heard, every terror that gripped you.'

Kavya felt her chest tighten.

Mark opened one of his drawers and took out a transparent plastic model of a red blood cell.

'Carbon monoxide binds to haemoglobin two hundred and forty times stronger than oxygen. It is a jealous gas. Once it enters the bloodstream, it clamps itself there, refusing to let go.' He clipped a tiny black bead onto the model. 'This is carboxyhaemoglobin. When this forms, oxygen cannot enter. Your brain starves. Slowly. Silently.'

He placed the model in front of her.

'Your brain is the first organ to scream when oxygen goes down. Even a slight drop in oxygen disrupts everything. Your sense of balance. Judgement. Vision. Sound. Memory. Mood. The world becomes distorted.'

He walked to the whiteboard and began to write.

CONFUSION

POOR JUDGEMENT

DREAD

DISORIENTATION

MEMORY GAPS

'These symptoms alone can mimic a hundred ghost stories,' he said.

He turned to her with a grave expression.

'You were suffocating, Kavya. Not enough to die yet but enough to see the world incorrectly.'

She shivered.

Mark dimmed the lights slightly and stood near a chart

that showed how oxygen flows to the brain.

'Now comes the frightening part,' he said. 'When the brain is starved, different regions misfire. Your visual cortex. Your auditory cortex. Your sensory cortex. They begin creating noise. Static. False images. Half-formed shadows.'

He flicked on his tablet screen. A diagram of the human brain appeared.

'Low oxygen makes your brain misinterpret shapes. So you saw flickering shadows in the corner of your eyes. The brain is tricked. It creates movement where none exists.'

He mimicked a flickering hand at the edge of her vision.

'That is why you saw someone standing just beyond your peripheral view. When you turned, it vanished. Because your eyes were working. But your brain was not.'

He moved to another diagram.

'Low oxygen also distorts hearing. If you hear a cloth rustle, your brain may tell you it is something crawling. If a pipe clicks, you may hear a knock. If someone walks upstairs, your brain transforms it into footsteps inside your room.'

Kavya stared at him with wide eyes.

'This is why you heard knocking sounds, soft sighs, faint footsteps in the corridor. These are classic CO hallucinations.'

He paced slowly, the sound of his shoes echoing in the quiet room.

'Now, why did all this happen with you?' he asked.

'Because I closed all windows,' Kavya whispered.

'Exactly. You trapped the gas inside. Carbon monoxide leaks silently. It is odourless, colourless, tasteless. It does not sting your eyes. It does not irritate your nose. It has no personality. It just kills when it likes.'

He sat on the edge of the table.

'When you closed the windows and tried to sleep, the concentration rose. As you slept, the oxygen levels in your brain dropped further. This is why you woke up feeling watched. Why you had terrifying dreams. Why you felt something sitting on your chest. Why you could not move.'

'Sleep paralysis,' murmured Jyolsna.

'Yes,' said Mark. 'But magnified by carbon monoxide. The brain wakes but the muscles do not. Combine that with oxygen deprivation and you get the feeling that someone is leaning over you.'

Kavya covered her face with her hands.

'You even saw the room tilt,' said Mark softly. 'That is the cerebellum misfiring. It controls balance. When oxygen is low, your brain cannot interpret space properly. It skews the world.'

He stepped closer.

'And then the hallucinations became bigger. More defined. More monstrous. Shadow people. Full shapes. Dark figures standing near the fridge or behind the door.'

He tapped a diagram of the fusiform gyrus.

'This,' he said, circling a small region behind the temple, 'is your fusiform gyrus. The part of your brain that recognises faces. It is one of the oldest and most sensitive systems we have. Humans are wired from birth to detect faces faster than anything else. Eyes. Mouth. Expressions. A threat. A smile. Anything that might save your life.'

He leaned back slightly, settling into professor mode.

'A long, long time ago, in the early stages of human evolution, it was vital to know if something was watching you. In the grasslands, in the forests, even in the dark. If you could quickly recognise a face, you survived. If you could not, a leopard or a rival tribe or a stranger in the woods got to you first. The ones who recognised faces fastest lived long enough to have children. That means our brains today are descendants of the most paranoid and most alert humans.'

Kavya watched him closely.

'The brain would rather see a face where there is none than miss a real danger,' Mark continued. 'This tendency is called pareidolia. Pattern recognition gone into overdrive. You look at clouds and see animals. You glance at a wall and see an old man's face. You see a woman's eyes in the folds of your curtains. Evolution designed you this way. It is safer to imagine a face than to miss one.'

He flipped a page in his notebook, revealing a rough sketch of a tiled bathroom wall.

'Under normal oxygen levels your fusiform gyrus works properly. It identifies only real faces. The moment oxygen begins to drop, the region misfires. It becomes desperate. It begins to interpret every pattern as a possible threat. Every stain on the wall becomes an eye. Every line becomes a mouth. The damp patch above your bed turns into a frowning face. And because the brain is stressed and dying for oxygen, those imagined faces look angry or twisted or hostile.'

He pointed at the sketch again.

'That is why you saw faces in tiles. That is why the shadows seemed to smile or glare. It was not a spirit trying to show itself. It was your brain doing exactly what evolution trained it to do. It tried to protect you. It tried to warn you. But it was working with too little oxygen and too much fear.'

He lowered his voice.

'Carbon monoxide does not just poison you. It hijacks millions of years of natural selection. It turns the brain's survival instincts against you. And that feels exactly like a haunting.'

Kavya swallowed hard, realising her terror had not come from outside her at all. It had come from the oldest part of being human. She gulped a breath and gripped the chair.

'The sense of presence,' said Mark. 'The most terrifying

symptom. That primal certainty that someone is in the room with you. Your amygdala fires like a malfunctioning alarm. You feel watched. Followed.' He paused. 'Hunted.'

Kavya trembled.

'All because your brain was suffocating.'

Mark moved to the far end of the room where a tall metal shelf leaned slightly to one side, burdened by decades of books that looked older than some university libraries. He ran his fingers along the cracked leather spines until he found a thick volume bound in dark brown, its edges frayed and its title barely readable. He pulled it out with both hands, dust rising in a faint cloud that shimmered in the lamplight.

'This,' he said, carrying it back to the table like an archaeologist revealing an ancient relic, 'is one of my favourites. A documented case. A proper one. Something that is still taught in forensic psychology.'

He opened the book.

The yellowed pages crackled like dry leaves. On one page was a black-and-white photograph of an old American house. A large timber building with a slanted roof, tall windows and a porch that sagged slightly, wrapped in fog.

He turned the book around so Kavya could see.

'This happened in 1912,' said Mark. 'A small rural town in USA. There was this old Victorian house which belonged to the Henderson family. A schoolteacher named Margaret Henderson lived there with her husband, Thomas and their two daughters.'

He tapped the photograph lightly.

'One winter, they began complaining about strange activity inside the house. Margaret wrote letters to the local sheriff saying she heard footsteps on the attic floor although no one lived above. Thomas claimed he saw shadows sliding across the parlour walls. The daughters said cold spots would appear in their rooms although the fireplace was burning. Then objects started moving. Chairs shifting an inch. A bowl turning on its own. Doors unlocking themselves.'

Kavya looked at the photographs of the book.

'The townsfolk believed the house was cursed,' continued Mark. 'They said the land was once used by travelling circuses in the nineteenth century and that a performer had died there. Some even claimed the property was built on old Cherokee mass burial site. Rumours grew. Fear multiplied. The Hendersons were terrified.'

He flipped the page.

The next photograph showed an investigator wearing a hat and holding a lantern, crouching beside an old furnace.

'This man,' said Mark, pointing, 'was Professor James Brewster. A chemist and an early environmental researcher. The sheriff asked him to examine the place because the Hendersons were nearly ready to abandon the house. Brewster spent a night there with his notebook. He experienced shadows moving at the edge of his vision. He felt the coldness. He heard faint knocks. But unlike the family, he stayed calm.'

Mark leaned forward.

'And do you know what he found?'

Kavya shook her head.

'The furnace which was used for heating during winter had a problem. It was in the basement and it had a cracked exhaust vent. Instead of sending smoke and fumes out of the chimney, it was leaking carbon monoxide into the living spaces. The gas filled the hallway, the bedrooms, even the attic. And since it was winter, all the windows were sealed tight. Every member of the family was being slowly poisoned.'

He turned the next page.

There was an old typewritten report.

'Professor Brewster concluded that every so-called

haunting was caused by carbon monoxide poisoning. The shadows they saw were visual hallucinations. The footsteps were auditory distortions. The cold spots were circulation issues. The moving objects were caused by dizziness and misinterpretations. The sense of being watched was the amygdala screaming from low oxygen. Once he fixed the furnace and allowed fresh air in, every single haunting disappeared.'

He looked up at Kavya.

'The Hendersons went back to living peacefully. No ghosts. No demons. Just breathable air.'

He closed the book with care.

'This case is still cited in forensic psychology and environmental medicine. It is one of the earliest documented examples of a haunting explained entirely by science. A house full of fear, saved by chemistry. It was published in 1921 in the American Journal of Ophthalmology by William Willmer.'

He placed the book down and met her eyes.

'Exactly like yours, Kavya.'

He shut the book with a soft thud.

'Carbon monoxide creates perfect haunted houses.'

'What about the cryptic messages of the post-it notes?' asked Kavya.

'Who wrote them. How they got inside a locked room,' asked Mark.

She tilted her head stiffly.

'You did.'

Kavya recoiled slightly. 'No. No, I did not. That handwriting is not mine. My hands don't shiver like this.'

'They do when you are half unconscious,' said Mark. His tone was calm. 'Sit with me for a minute and I'll show you.'

He pulled a chair closer. Kavya sat down slowly, eyes fixed on the note.

Mark continued, 'When carbon monoxide binds to your blood, your brain gets less oxygen. That means your consciousness flickers. You drift in and out of awareness. You may look awake. You may even walk, open drawers, boil water, unlock doors or write things. But your mind is not fully present. You are in a twilight state. Neither dreaming nor fully awake.'

He leaned forward.

'That is dissociation caused by hypoxia. CO poisoning turns your brain into a dimming torch. It flickers. It sputters. It tries to stay on. In those moments you can act without forming memories.'

Kavya whispered, 'So I wrote them in my sleep?'

'Not sleep,' said Mark. 'A kind of semi-consciousness. It feels like sleepwalking. But your eyes are open. Your coordination is off. Your hands shiver. Your fine motor control collapses. That is why the handwriting looks crooked and unfamiliar. Those notes I saw were classic hypoxic handwriting. Uneven pressure. Slanted words. Letters that drift upward or downward. No proper spacing. A healthy person cannot write like this unless they are trembling violently.'

'But I do not remember writing it,' she said, her voice hollow.

'Of course not,' replied Mark. 'The hippocampus, the part of your brain that forms memories, shuts down first when oxygen is low. So anything you do during a CO episode goes into a void. You can write messages, move objects, even talk aloud and you will remember none of it.'

Kavya rubbed her neck, horrified. 'But why would I write something like this? Why would I warn myself?'

'Because your brain knew something was wrong,' said Mark. 'Even in that semi-conscious state, your body recognised the danger. Your subconscious tried to communicate with your conscious mind. Those notes were not predictions or supernatural warnings. They were distress signals from your own brain.'

Tears welled in Kavya's eyes, not from fear but from the slow, dawning horror that her own body had been struggling to stay alive while she thought a ghost stalked her.

Mark began listing symptoms on the board while speaking.

'Shadow figures. Whispers. Feeling pushed. Sudden terror. Cold spots. Nightmares. Memory lapses. Mood swings. Irritability. Depression.'

He turned to her.

'You experienced every single one.'

Silence filled the room.

Kavya finally asked in a trembling voice, 'So everything was a lie my brain made up?'

Mark sat beside her, careful not to startle her.

'Not a lie. A misinterpretation. A drowning mind that was trying to understand why it could not breathe.'

Kavya began to cry. Jyolsna placed a hand on her shoulder. Mark poured her a glass of water.

'You were not haunted by ghosts,' he said softly. 'You were haunted by chemistry.'

He stood and walked to the corner of the room where he kept a small metal model of a chimney.

'Will it go away now?' she asked weakly.

'Yes,' said Mark. 'The building management will unblock the shaft. The generator will be moved. Proper ventilation will be installed. Once the gas stops, the ghosts will stop.'

Mark leaned back in his chair, studying Kavya's face with a seriousness that made her stomach knot.

He spoke quietly. 'Kavya, you need to understand how close you came. This is not exaggeration. If you had stayed in that flat for another month, you would not be here.'

'I... I thought the ghost was the danger,' Kavya murmured.

'No,' said Mark. 'It was the gas. And it was killing you from the moment you moved in.'

He clasped his hands and leaned forward.

'Do you know what would have happened next? You would stop waking up,' said Mark.

Kavya shivered.

'Not dramatically. Not like the films. You would simply fall asleep one night. Your brain would be too oxygen deprived to scream. Your body would be too weak to fight. Your lungs would slow down. Your heart would flutter a few times, like a dying bird. Then it would stop.'

Kavya's fingers gripped the arm of the chair.

'The neighbours would find you after a day or two,' Mark went on, voice low. 'The post-it notes scattered. The windows closed. The gas still trapped. And everyone would call it a tragic accident. Or maybe a suicide. You would become a small news item. Nothing more.'

Kavya covered her mouth. Tears leaked down her cheeks.

'But you were lucky,' said Mark. 'You fainted on the stairs. You fell out of the gas pocket. That fall may have saved your life. If that had not happened...'

He let the sentence hang.

Kavya whispered, 'So if I had stayed a few more weeks...'

'A few more weeks,' repeated Mark softly, 'and you would have died in your sleep. The brain cannot survive long-term hypoxia. People in CO-filled rooms slowly lose consciousness and never wake again. You were already having severe hallucinations, sleep paralysis, memory lapses. Those are the final warnings.'

He took a breath.

She wept silently, shoulders trembling.

'I paid money to a man who said it was a jinn,' she

whispered.

'Kavya, I want you to understand something important. What happened to you is not rare. What is rare is that you got the right help before you were seriously harmed. People like Rashid… they thrive on situations exactly like yours.'

Kavya looked up. 'He seemed so convincing.'

'Of course he did,' Mark replied. 'Fear makes people vulnerable. And fear mixed with physical symptoms makes people desperate.'

He leaned back slightly.

'And this is where people like Rashid enter. They study fear the way doctors study anatomy. They know what frightened people want to hear. They know what frightened people are willing to believe. They create a script and they repeat it for every victim.'

'So they lie?' Kavya asked softly.

'They do worse than lie,' said Mark. 'They weaponise psychology. In most cases, the problems people face are temporary. Anxiety. Stress. Sleep deprivation. Loneliness. A creaking pipe. A rat in the ceiling. A flickering light. These are simple, natural things.'

He tapped the table in quiet emphasis as he spoke.

'Then the sorcerer enters with his theatrics. Chanting. Smoke. Powder. Holy water. Dramatic warnings about jinns or spirits. And because the victim expects healing and because the symptoms were going to subside anyway, the person feels better. Placebo takes care of the rest.'

Kavya lowered her head slowly.

'So they look genuine,' she said.

'Exactly,' replied Mark. 'And once they fix two or three simple problems by coincidence, they become confident. They start believing they truly have supernatural powers. But the truth is simple. Most psychological disturbances settle on their own. They only need reassurance, not rituals.'

He paused, then continued in a quieter voice.

'But cases like yours are different. Carbon monoxide poisoning is not psychological. It is not spiritual. It is chemical. Biological. Physical. And that is why Rashid's theatrics did nothing. They cannot fix oxygen deprivation. They cannot stop haemoglobin binding to carbon monoxide. They cannot repair a brain that is being suffocated.'

Kavya lowered her eyes.

'He said he could repel the spirit,' she whispered.

Mark sighed. 'He cannot repel a molecule. He cannot chant a gas out of your lungs. He cannot sprinkle water on carbon monoxide and make it flee. And that is what makes these situations dangerous. Additionally, his smoke treatment made worse by releasing more carbon monoxide in the room.'

Mark stretched his arms over his head.

'If you had continued with Rashid's methods, you would have died. Not because of ghosts. But because you would have delayed the only real solution, which was fixing the ventilation and getting out of that room. Carbon monoxide does not care about rituals. It does not care about chants. It does not fear magical powders from Yemen. It kills quietly. And only science stops it.'

Kavya breathed out shakily. 'I feel stupid.'

'No,' said Mark softly. 'Fear makes us look for explanations. When you are terrified and alone, anyone who speaks with confidence can sound like a saviour. You are not stupid. You were frightened. And someone took advantage of that.'

She wiped her eyes.

'So… I was not going crazy.'

'Not at all,' said Mark. 'You were being poisoned.'

Mark sighed. 'It is common. When the brain feels something unnatural, it reaches for supernatural explanations.

People like him exploit that fear. Fear is currency for such men.'

He looked at her with seriousness.

'You are safe now,' he said.

Kavya slumped slightly, her fear giving way to a mixture of awe and exhaustion.

'Thank you, doctor,' she said.

Mark smiled faintly.

'Come,' he said. 'Ashok will drive you home. And keep your windows open tonight. There won't be any dust and noise pollution at night. After eleven months, you may shift the apartment if you wish.'

'I don't know how to thank you,' said Kavya, with a gesture of prayer.

'The ghost hunting fees is one lakh Rupees,' Ashok chuckled. 'EMI option is available.'

Jyolsna laughed.

'Don't worry about it,' said Mark. 'Trust science.'

Kavya stepped out of the house, feeling the fresh air on her face for the first time in days, as though breathing had finally become a natural act again. Outside, the sky had darkened and a soft wind rustled the leaves. The street lamps flickered on.

She looked up at the night sky.

Nothing watched her.

Nothing followed her.

Nothing whispered in the dark.

Only silence.

Only air.

Only life returning.

CHAPTER FOUR
Holding the Line

Three cameras stood like quiet sentinels. One framed the entire set, catching the minimalist setting, the microphones, the cups of untouched coffee. Another stayed on Satyajit, who reclined in his chair with the relaxed confidence of someone who enjoyed provoking thought. The third remained fixed on Dr Mark.

Red lights blinked on.

'So, Dr Mark, what do you have to say about the controversy you have landed yourself in lately?' Satyajit smiled into the camera.

Mark adjusted his posture, fingers loosely intertwined. 'Can you specify?' he said with a soft chuckle. 'I seem to have collected quite a few controversies.'

'The one about religion. There have been a lot of online rants claiming that a doctor like you should not publicly criticise religion or God.'

'What to say. Things happen,' Mark replied tilting his head slightly. 'It was during a speech I delivered at the university. I was talking about how religions evolved. I think what upset people was my statement that all holy books were written by humans. I assumed that was common sense. Apparently, it still is not.'

'So they were not written by some superior force in the sky?' Satyajit raised an eyebrow theatrically.

'Of course not,' Mark said calmly. 'Isn't it obvious? Every holy book is written in a local language. Sanskrit, Hebrew, Arabic. If an all powerful being wanted to communicate with humanity, wouldn't there be a universal language? Wouldn't the text be accessible to everyone equally, without translations and interpretations?'

'That actually makes a lot of sense.' Satyajit nodded slowly.

'And if you look closely,' Mark brought himself forward slightly. 'You can see how religions evolved from older belief systems. Regional myths, tribal deities, local legends. All of them get absorbed and refined over time.'

He paused, choosing his words carefully.

'Take Hinduism, for example. Long before it became what we know today, there were countless regional belief systems. Hunter gatherer tribes who migrated from Africa worshipped nature, animals, spirits. Later, agricultural communities from regions like ancient Iran contributed their own deities and rituals. Then came the Proto Indo European tribes, bringing gods like Indra and Rudra. Over centuries, everything mixed together and eventually formed the Vedic religion and what we now broadly call Hinduism.'

Satyajit listened intently.

'What is unique,' Mark continued, 'is that Hinduism did not erase the older gods. It absorbed them. That is why it has such a vast pantheon. It accommodated belief instead of annihilating it.'

'What about the Abrahamic religions?' Satyajit asked.

Mark smiled. 'That is another fascinating subject. Scholars have studied the Bible and the Torah in great detail. We know roughly when each part was written. The earliest texts date back to around nine hundred BCE. Genesis was not written by one person in one sitting. It evolved over time. At that time, several tribes lived in the region. Some were even named after the gods they worshipped, like Asher or Gad. The Sea Peoples from Greece later became the Philistines and influenced local myths. You can see parallels between Samson and Hercules if you read carefully.'

'That is not something people like to hear.' Satyajit laughed softly. 'And if you tread further to other religions, there might be chances of getting your hand or head cut off."

'Unfortunately, yes,' Mark replied. 'This is a massive topic. I am not a historian, but I find it deeply fascinating. Once you understand how religions evolved as cultural systems, without attaching blind divinity to them, you become more informed and far less fanatical. In my university speech, I barely scratched the surface. It is time consuming and frankly not my field. But all the research is available online for anyone willing to look.'

'That brings me to another question. Despite holding such views, why are you not part of the Atheist Society?' asked Satyajit.

'Because I do not consider myself an atheist. I still go to temples.'

'You do? So you pray?' Satyajit blinked.

'No,' Mark replied gently. 'I do not pray asking for favours. That never works. I go to temples to absorb the atmosphere. To chant slokas that venerate ideals rather than demand blessings. I admire the architecture, the sculptures, the philosophy.'

Mark paused with thoughtful eyes. 'Many concepts in

Hindu philosophy still align surprisingly well with modern science. Even scientists like Carl Sagan acknowledged that ancient Indian cosmology coincidentally mirrors some modern discoveries. It means it is worth studying.'

The room fell into a reflective silence for a moment.

'So you are not rejecting religion entirely,' Satyajit said.

'No,' Mark replied. 'I am rejecting blind belief. There is a difference.'

The conversation flowed on, touching on science, fear, superstition and responsibility. When the recording finally ended, the red light on the cameras went dark.

The city had begun to loosen its grip on the night as Ashok guided the car out of the narrow studio lane and onto the broader road. Traffic was thinner now, reduced to the occasional bus sighing past or a motorbike cutting through the air like an insect.

Ashok glanced at Mark briefly before returning his eyes to the road. 'So when can we expect this video to be aired?'

'Knowing Satyajit, he will edit it quickly. Probably next week. It will go up on his YouTube channel.' Mark smiled faintly.

'Do you usually watch your interviews later?' Ashok asked.

'No,' Mark replied without hesitation. 'I never do.'

'That is actually a very good habit. Otherwise you will end up reading the comments.' Ashok chuckled.

Mark turned his head and looked at Ashok properly now. 'I never read comments. Not because they are always negative, though many of them are. It is more about understanding human behaviour.'

'Meaning?' Ashok raised an eyebrow.

'People derive pleasure from being cruel when there are no consequences,' Mark said calmly. 'Anonymity gives them courage. I talk about beliefs and the supernatural. Naturally that challenges some people, so they react. But I have seen worse. Absolute venom under videos of someone cooking a simple dish or singing an old song or explaining how to grow plants.'

'You're right,' said Ashok.

'It is not about disagreement. It is about power. The power to wound someone without ever facing them. That is why cyber bullying thrives. I do not need that kind of noise in my head.'

'Yep. Silence is better.' Ashok gave a small, confirming tilt of his head.

The car rolled over a patch of uneven road, causing a soft jolt. Mark's phone vibrated in his pocket almost immediately. He glanced at the screen.

'Meena,' he said and exhaled quietly.

Ashok gave him a knowing look. 'That psycho atheist lady again.'

Mark answered the phone which was connected to the car. 'Hello.'

'Hi, doc,' Meena's voice came through the speakers of the car.

'Yes, Meena. Tell me,' Mark replied.

'I am calling to invite you to take part in a programme our organisation is conducting next week,' she said.

'What is it about?' Mark straightened slightly.

'It is a protest event,' Meena said. 'As you know, the Sabarimala temple does not allow menstruating women to enter. This is blatant misogyny. It goes against everything a progressive society stands for. We are organising a programme to address this issue.'

Mark remained silent, letting her speak.

'We may even mobilise a group of young women to forcefully enter Sabarimala,' Meena continued. 'As a public intellectual and someone who actively debunks superstition, it is important that you stand with us.'

Mark closed his eyes briefly. 'I am sorry,' he said at last. 'I will not be taking part in it.'

There was a pause on the other end.

'Why?' Meena asked sharply.

'I do not have a problem with that particular rule of the Sabarimala temple,' Mark replied.

Ashok glanced sideways, sensing the shift in tone.

'So you are a misogynist too now?' Meena snapped.

'If it were misogyny, the temple would not allow women at all. The restriction applies only to menstruating women between the ages of twelve and sixty.'

'It is misogyny regardless,' Meena insisted.

'Tell me something, Meena. Are you a believer in Lord Ayyappa?' Mark sighed.

'Of course not,' she said. 'I am an atheist.'

'Then tell me,' Mark said, 'do you think any true believer of Ayyappa who happens to be a menstruating woman actually wants to visit that temple?'

There was a brief silence. Then Meena scoffed. 'Those backward believers are running a ridiculous "ready to wait" campaign anyway.'

'In that case,' Mark replied, 'you have no right to interfere with their traditions. The temple exists within its own premises. It functions on donations from believers. As long as that is the case, it has the right to follow its traditions. And the believers themselves seem to have no problem following those rules. I believe such matters should be decided by the devotees, not imposed by atheists who do not believe in the deity to begin with.'

'You are speaking like a true conservative fascist,' Meena said coldly.

'If that is how you see it, then so be it,' Mark said.

He ended the call.

For a few moments, only the sound of the engine and the faint hiss of tyres on the road filled the car. Ashok slowed down as they approached the signal and stopped.

Ashok cleared his throat. 'That was intense.'

Mark nodded. 'It always is when belief and identity collide.'

'Do you think she will drag you into another controversy over this?' Ashok asked.

'Probably,' Mark said. 'But that is not my concern. I do not take positions to please people. I take them because I believe they are intellectually honest.'

The signal turned green. Ashok pressed the accelerator and the car moved forward again.

'It is strange,' Ashok said after a while. 'You debunk ghosts, gods and superstitions, yet people from both sides get angry at you.'

Mark smiled faintly. 'That is the price of refusing to belong to any camp. If you do not chant slogans, everyone assumes you are against them.'

He leaned back again, watching the city recede. 'Most people do not want understanding. They want validation. The moment you deny that, you become the enemy.'

Ashok said nothing. He knew Mark well enough to understand that these were not complaints. They were observations.

The car turned into a quieter road lined with trees. Their shadows stretched across the pavement. Mark felt the exhaustion settle deeper into his bones. The interview, the call, the constant need to explain himself.

*

The smell of fried paneer and toasted flour lingered in

Mark's house long after the stove had been turned off. Mark stood at the kitchen counter, dusting his hands and stacking the last chapati onto a steel plate, while Ashok stirred the paneer chilli with exaggerated care.

'Careful,' Mark said, glancing sideways. 'If you burn the paneer, I will pretend not to know you.'

'Relax, King Nala,' Ashok replied.

They carried the plates to the living room and sat on the couch before the television. The cricket match was nearing its final overs, tension thick in the air. Ashok came forward eyes glued to the screen. Mark reclined against the sofa and began chewing thoughtfully.

India won with a dramatic boundary.

Ashok jumped up, pumping his fist.

The happiness was small, uncomplicated and deeply comforting. On nights like these, Ashok did not return to his house where he lived with his parents. Mark never needed to ask him to stay. The guest bedroom existed precisely for such evenings.

They cleaned up together, moving around each other with the familiarity of people who had done this many times before. When they finally retired to their rooms, the house felt lighter.

Morning announced itself with the hiss of batter hitting hot iron.

Mark padded into the kitchen to find Ashok standing over the stove, expertly spreading dosa batter in widening circles.

'You are spoiling me,' Mark said.

'Slight ghee consumption won't give you cholesterol,' Ashok replied.

Mark added coconut, green chillies and ginger into the jar and switched it on. The kitchen filled with the sharp, comforting aroma of chutney in the making. They spoke over the noise, sentences broken and resumed between flips of dosa and the whirr of the blender. The tea was already prepared.

'So,' Mark said casually, 'you can take two weeks off.'

Ashok froze mid flip. 'What?'

Mark turned off the blender and looked at him. 'Relax.'

'Why would I relax?' Ashok asked. 'Two weeks off sounds suspicious.'

'I am going to my village,' Mark said. 'To the tharavadu. Gotta attend the festival of our family temple.'

'Oh. It is that time of the year.' Ashok's shoulders loosened.

'Yes. I will be going with my brother and his family.'

Ashok resumed flipping the dosa. 'So where exactly is this place?'

'A small village in Pathanamthitta district.'

'So that makes you a migrant from Pathanamthitta,' Ashok nodded thoughtfully.

'If you want to simplify it,' Mark smiled.

'Your ancestors are from there.'

'Some of them,' Mark said. 'About two hundred and fifty years ago, my ancestors migrated there from Malabar.'

'Why?' Ashok raised an eyebrow.

Mark poured the chutney into a bowl before answering. 'Hyder Ali's invasions. Muslim armies from Mysore swept through Malabar. Nair nobles and their families were attacked, pillaged, massacred. Those who survived fled. The King of Travancore gave them asylum. Many settled in Pathanamthitta.'

'So originally Malabar,' Ashok absorbed this quietly.

'Not quite,' Mark said. 'Anthropologically, the Nair community is believed to have origins near the Godavari river banks. Possibly Andhra Telangana.'

'So Andhra ancestors,' Ashok laughed.

'Still not quite,' Mark replied patiently. 'Those communities themselves were migrants from the Gangetic plains. Early agricultural societies.'

'So modern day Uttar Pradesh,' Ashok chewed his dosa slowly.

'Before that,' Mark continued, unfazed, 'they came from the Indus Valley civilisation. Northwest India. Modern day Pakistan. Around 2500 BCE.'

'Let me guess. Before that, Iran,' Ashok held up a hand.

'Correct,' Mark said. 'Descendants of people who discovered agricultural technology from Mesopotamia. Euphrates and Tigris. About seven thousand years ago.'

'Why not Iraq while we are at it,' Ashok grinned.

'Eventually Africa,' Mark said. 'Botswana region. Forty to sixty thousand years ago.'

'Fine. African ancestors. Mine too,' Ashok laughed aloud.

Mark gave a small, confirming gesture. 'Exactly.'

'So we are relatives,' Ashok said. 'Despite different castes and all that nonsense.'

'Yes,' Mark said.

Ashok grew thoughtful. 'Wish everyone thought like this.'

Mark shifted back against the counter. 'Nothing would change. Humans have always killed their own kind. Tribe, clan, religion. Violence is not erased by shared ancestry.'

'That is where philosophy comes in. Psychology too.' Ashok shrugged.

'Speaking of which, why did you never pursue psychology after graduation?' Mark looked at him closely.

Ashok flipped the last dosa. 'There were only BA Psychology seats left when I joined. Government gave everyone A plus. College allocation was chaos. My mentors said Masters, then PhD, then teach. Sounded like a pyramid scheme.'

Mark chuckled.

'Then I became your assistant,' Ashok continued. 'And suddenly life became interesting. Dangerous. Weird. Like a movie. Maybe I will write a book someday.'

'Make sure you portray me as tall and handsome.' Mark laughed openly.

Ashok bowed dramatically.

'The Casebook of a Paranormal Investigator!' said Ashok. 'How does that sound?'

'I'll take 95 per cent of the royalty,' said Mark.

'In that case, you write it yourself,' chuckled Ashok.

'Na, I prefer a ghostwriter,' said Mark.

'How about the title, "The Ghost Hunter: Written by a Ghostwriter"?' asked Ashok.

'That's catchy,' replied Mark.

It took another half an hour to finish the breakfast.

Ashok left in the late afternoon. Mark handed him a small envelope and a paper bag.

'What is this?' Ashok asked.

'Money,' Mark said simply. 'And some things you might need. Go somewhere. Travel. Waste time. Eat badly. Come back with stories.'

'You make it sound like an order,' Ashok laughed, but his eyes softened.

'It is,' Mark replied. 'And don't argue.'

Ashok exhaled, then gave a slight tilt of his head. 'Take care, doc.'

'You too.'

The motorcycle disappeared. Mark closed the door slowly shifting his mind to the journey ahead.

A couple of hours later, he was behind the wheel of his brother's car, an ageing but well maintained sedan. Viswamitran sat beside him, relaxed but already complaining. In the back seat, Sulekha watched the road with mild curiosity while their two sons were lost in the glow of their smartphones.

'You have no idea how difficult it was to get leave,' Viswamitran said. 'The office is a battlefield. Everyone wants credit. No one wants responsibility.'

'You work in beverages. Not diplomacy,' Mark nodded.

'Same thing these days. Politics everywhere,' Viswamitran snorted.

For three hours, the road unwound itself from city congestion into narrower highways and then into village roads shaded by rubber trees and coconut palms. The air grew cleaner. The sky widened. Even the children looked up occasionally.

When they finally turned into the familiar road, Mark slowed the car instinctively. The tharavadu rose before them, its tiled roof darkened by age, its wooden pillars standing firm like silent elders. The central courtyard lay open to the sky, a square of earth and sunlight that had once echoed with laughter, arguments, prayers and footsteps now long gone.

Their parents had died long ago, one after the other, leaving behind memories thick enough to feel tangible. Viswamitran and Mark had never considered selling the house. It was not merely property. It was a map of who they were.

They had restored it carefully, refusing to modernise it into something unrecognisable. A caretaker lived nearby, keeping it clean, opening it occasionally to travellers who wanted to experience village life without turning it into spectacle.

The car door had barely closed when neighbours began arriving. A distant cousin. An old family friend. A neighbour who remembered Mark as a boy who asked too many questions. Chairs were pulled out. Coffee appeared. Conversations drifted lazily from health to crops to politics.

The children sat apart, shoulders hunched, fingers tapping

endlessly.

Mark watched them for a moment, then stood and walked into one of the inner rooms. He returned holding an old cricket bat, its handle wrapped in fraying tape and a faded rubber ball.

'Come,' he said to the boys. 'Front yard. Five overs.'

They barely looked up.

'Later, uncle' one muttered.

Mark sighed and turned to Viswamitran. 'You?'

Viswamitran laughed. 'I will collapse before the first ball.'

The bat went back into the room, gathering dust once more.

As evening approached, the mood shifted subtly. The temple trustees arrived, their expressions seemed formal and rehearsed. Kuttan, the most vocal among them, stepped forward with a folded receipt.

'Here,' he said, handing it over. 'The receipt of your contribution to the festival fund.'

Viswamitran examined it and passed it to Mark.

'We also need four lakhs more,' Kuttan added quickly. 'We collected one from the villagers. Three more pending.'

Mark looked up. 'For what?'

'Malayinkotta Prabhakaran,' Kuttan said with reverence.

'A film star?' Mark frowned.

'No, sir. An elephant. A famous one.'

Mark stared at him. 'Since when did we need celebrity elephants?'

'Every temple does it now,' Kuttan said defensively. 'And fireworks. Plavinkodu Bhagavaty Temple had a grand display last month. Huge crowd.'

'Maybe we can manage some amount,' Viswamitran shifted uncomfortably.

'No,' Mark said quietly.

'Sir, this is culture. You're an atheist. You don't know.' Kuttan blinked.

'Culture does not mean imitation. Did our temple ever have elephants?' Mark's voice sharpened. 'A hundred years ago, the handful of temples in Kerala that used elephants for festivals relied on animals that were local. They lived nearby. They walked to the temple. Their bodies and minds were accustomed to the land, the sounds, the people. There was no chaos forced upon them.'

He paused, letting the image settle.

'That world no longer exists. Today, tens of thousands of temples want elephants for their festivals and only a very small number of them are available. The same few animals are dragged from place to place like travelling props. They are stuffed into lorries, driven at high speeds for hours, sometimes days. That alone is enough to disrupt their biological balance. Their sleep cycle breaks. Their stress hormones spike. Their instincts go into survival mode.'

His eyes hardened.

'And then we unload them into madness. Blaring film songs. Fireworks. Laser lights slicing through the night. Crowds screaming, pushing, climbing over one another. To us, it is celebration. To the elephant, it is a threat from every direction.'

Mark shook his head slowly.

'A frightened animal that weighs several tonnes does not become divine. It becomes dangerous. Confused. Unpredictable. And when it panics, it does the only thing its body knows how to do. It charges.'

He looked around again.

'How many times have we read the same news? Elephant runs amok during temple festival. Devotees injured. Lives lost. Committees express regret. A few days of outrage. And then nothing changes.'

His voice dropped, heavy with disappointment.

'We are not preserving tradition. We are manufacturing tragedy and calling it faith. And the worst part is, even after all this blood, people still refuse to learn.'

Kuttan hesitated.

'And about fireworks. Did our traditions ever have fireworks?' Mark continued. 'If we had gunpowder traditions, we would not have been colonised by the Portuguese or the British.'

Silence fell heavy.

'You wasted money last year on a film celebrity without consulting us,' Mark said. 'And now elephants. Tomorrow what? DJs? Fashion show?'

'People expect celebration,' Kuttan said weakly.

'People expect spectacle because you trained them to,' Mark replied. 'Our temple was simple. It was meant for reflection. Learning. Support.'

Mark stepped closer. 'I told you to raise funds for scholarships. For books. For children of devotees. You ignored it. Temples were once centres of knowledge. Now you are turning them into noise.'

Kuttan opened his mouth.

'No,' Mark said firmly. 'Cancel the unnecessary expenses. This is a festival, not a film award ceremony.'

Kuttan left, shoulders slumped.

Viswamitran looked troubled. 'Aren't these things part of the vibe now?'

'Not for our temple,' Mark replied. 'Give me one more year. Then I will place people who understand purpose over popularity.'

The night settled around the tharavadu. Mark stood in the courtyard, looking up at the open sky, thinking of generations that had stood exactly where he stood, arguing, believing, changing, resisting.

Some things, he knew, were worth holding the line for.

The morning sun fell softly on the tiled roofs of the tharavadu. Three days remained before the festival, yet the temple was already alive. Bells rang softly. Oil lamps flickered though the day had begun. The smell of incense, camphor and crushed flowers hung in the air like an old memory.

Mark walked barefoot along the stone pathway, the cool surface grounding him. Viswamitran walked beside him, hands folded loosely, greeting familiar faces with polite nods. Temple staff moved with practised ease, arranging flowers, preparing offerings, murmuring prayers that had been repeated for centuries without anyone remembering who first spoke them.

They completed the usual poojas, standing with heads bowed while the priest chanted mantras that rose and fell like waves. Mark watched closely, not with devotion but with observation. He had always believed that rituals revealed more about people than about gods. The way hands trembled while offering flowers. The way eyes closed too tightly when praying for something desperate. The way lips moved faster when fear crept in.

After the poojas, Viswamitran drifted away into conversation with an elderly trustee. Mark stayed back. He liked standing in temples when no one was paying attention to him. It gave him space to watch.

Devotees came and went. Some prayed silently. Some cried openly. Some whispered demands into stone ears, convinced that divinity worked best when treated like a bargaining clerk. Mark spoke briefly to a few villagers who recognised him, exchanged polite words, listened more than he spoke.

That was when he noticed the man and the child.

The man was young, perhaps thirty. The boy beside him looked no more than four. His head was shaven clean, the skin pale and vulnerable beneath the harsh daylight. His eyes wandered, curious and unfocused, unaware of the significance adults had burdened him with.

Mark felt a familiar tightening in his chest.

The man performed a hurried pooja, hands moving with rehearsed urgency. He smeared vibhuti on the child's forehead, then turmeric, then vermilion, his fingers leaving thick streaks of colour on soft skin. The boy winced but did not cry. He had already learned that obedience brought less pain.

Mark followed them at a distance when the man led the child outside the sanctum. He positioned himself near a stone pillar.

The man turned the child towards the temple, murmuring words under his breath. Then he reached into his shirt pocket and pulled out a pack of camphor blocks.

Mark's breath caught.

The man placed the white blocks into the child's open palm. The boy frowned, confused, staring at the unfamiliar object resting on his small hand.

Mark saw the matchbox.

Time slowed.

Mark stepped forward, his voice sharp and cutting through the hum of the temple courtyard.

'What are you doing?'

The man spun around, startled, instinctively pulling the child closer. His eyes flashed with irritation.

'Please do not interfere,' he said. 'I am doing what must be done.'

'You are about to burn the child's hand,' Mark said angrily.

'It is necessary,' the man replied. 'It is the only way.'

Mark reached out and, with quiet firmness, removed the

camphor from the child's palm. The boy looked up at him, surprised.

The raised voices drew attention. Devotees paused. A few murmurs rippled through the courtyard. The chief priest approached.

'What is happening, Rajiv?' the priest asked.

'This idiot is blocking my ritual,' the young man snapped. 'Who is he to interfere?'

Mark remained silent.

The priest looked at him and his tone softened. 'He is no idiot. This temple belongs to his family. He is Dr Markandeyan. A scholar. A scientist. We respect him.'

Rajiv scoffed. 'Whoever he is, he has no solution to my problem. Please tell him to step aside. I want peace in my life.'

Mark studied Rajiv closely. Beneath the anger was exhaustion. Fear had hollowed his eyes.

'What problem requires you to hurt your child to find peace?' Mark asked quietly.

Rajiv's voice cracked despite his attempt to sound firm. 'My son is followed by a ghost. A famous tantri told me this ritual will stop it. Can you solve my problem, Mr. Scientist. Can you get rid of the ghost?'

'As a matter of fact, I can,' replied Dr Mark.

CHAPTER FIVE
The Devil

Mark's tharavadu was quiet in the afternoon. Rajiv sat on the edge of the sofa, stiff-backed, his hands clasped together as though he were holding himself in place. His son sat beside him, legs dangling, eyes roaming curiously across the room. The boy seemed calmer here, Mark noticed. His gaze did not dart nervously to corners or shadows.

Mark took a seat opposite them with a notebook resting loosely on his knee. He had already asked his usual questions, the ones he asked in almost every case. Ventilation. Cooking fuel. Nearby generators. Old wiring. Dampness. Headaches. Dizziness. Nightmares. The answers had ruled out the most obvious culprit.

This was not carbon monoxide.

Mark closed the notebook and reclined back slightly, studying Rajiv with quiet focus.

'Tell me about yourself, Rajiv,' he said politely. 'I have not seen you around here before.'

Rajiv shifted, cleared his throat. 'My native place is north of here,' he began. 'I got married five years ago. Things did not go well in my parents' house. Too many relatives, too many opinions. So my wife and I rented a house here and started living here alone.'

He paused, glancing at his son, then continued.

'I work in Maldives. I come home once or twice a year, sometimes less. This time I could only manage two weeks.'

Mark studied him for a moment. 'And your son. When did he first start talking about seeing this… ghost?'

Rajiv exhaled slowly. 'Six months ago. That was when I came home last time. He told me then. I thought it was imagination. An imaginary friend. Children make up stories, don't they?'

The boy swung his feet, listening quietly.

'But this time,' Rajiv said, 'it is different. He describes it clearly. He points. He cries. He refuses to sleep alone. And I am leaving again soon. I will not be back for at least another year. I could not leave without fixing this.'

Mark's gaze softened. 'So you consulted a sorcerer.'

Rajiv nodded. 'By phone. He said the child is being followed by a ghost. He told me to do the ritual at the temple. I was desperate.'

Mark was silent for a moment, then asked, 'Do you believe in ghosts, Rajiv?'

Rajiv looked surprised. 'Yes. Of course. Everyone has a soul, right? Sometimes souls refuse to leave after death. They stay back. They haunt people. That is what ghosts are.'

Mark tilted his head slightly. 'You are a Hindu believer?'

'Yes,' Rajiv replied without hesitation.

'Then you do not need to worry about ghosts,' Mark said calmly.

Rajiv blinked. 'What do you mean?'

'There are no ghosts in Hinduism.'

For a moment, Rajiv stared at him, unsure whether he had heard correctly.

'What are you saying?' he asked. 'Ghosts will not attack Hindus?'

'No,' Mark said. 'I am saying something more basic. There is no concept of a ghost in Hinduism.'

Rajiv frowned. 'Then maybe the ghost is Christian. Or Muslim.'

Mark almost smiled. 'That is not what I meant.'

He leaned forward now.

'Have you ever read the Vedas? The Puranas? The Ramayana? The Mahabharata? Have you ever seen a mention of ghost in any of it?'

Rajiv hesitated. 'No. I have watched the serials. Ramayana, Mahabharata, Sivapurana. Thinking about it… yes. There were no ghosts in them.'

'Exactly,' Mark said. 'I have read them. All of them. There is no mention of bodiless souls wandering around to haunt the living.'

Rajiv's brow furrowed deeper.

'In Hinduism,' Mark continued, 'when a person dies, the soul is reborn. Reincarnation. Again and again. Very rarely, an enlightened soul attains moksha and is liberated. There is no in-between state where the soul hangs around as a ghost.'

He paused to let that sink in.

'There is mention of *parakayapravesha* in ancient plays. Souls entering another body. But not wandering without a body. The idea of ghosts is a Western import.'

Rajiv sat back, processing.

'But Yakshis,' he said suddenly. 'The revenge-seeking female ghosts. They are real, right?'

Mark replied evenly, 'Yakshis are divine beings in Hinduism. Guardians of sacred groves. That is why Yakshi deities are worshipped in temples. When European horror literature entered Kerala in the nineteenth century and influenced the people here, local writers borrowed the word and reshaped it to fit ghost stories.'

Rajiv looked unsettled. 'What about Kalliyankaatu Neeli?'

'That legend is older,' Mark agreed. 'But the original texts describe reincarnation. A woman reborn, taking revenge in another life. Not a ghost.'

Rajiv was quiet for a long moment.

'So you do not believe me,' he said finally. 'Or my child.'

Mark shook his head. 'I believe your fear. And I believe your child's experience.'

He looked at the boy, who was now watching him intently.

'I was only explaining philosophy,' Mark said softly. 'Belief systems matter. They shape how fear grows.'

Rajiv's shoulders slumped slightly. 'Then how can you help us if you don't believe in us?'

Mark folded his hands. 'Don't worry. I believe you. I have the tools and gadgets to hunt ghosts. I'll help you.'

Rajiv let out a breath he seemed to have been holding for months.

'Thank you,' he said quietly.

The boy looked up at Mark and, for the first time, smiled.

*

Rajiv's house stood at the end of a narrow lane, half-hidden by overgrown shrubs and a crooked jackfruit tree. The paint on the walls had faded unevenly under years of sun and rain. It was not an old house, not ancient enough to inspire legends, yet it had the quiet loneliness of a place lived in cautiously.

Mark stepped out of his car and paused for a moment, taking in the surroundings. He listened. There was no unusual silence, no oppressive stillness. Just the distant bark of a dog, the rhythmic clang of a vessel from a neighbouring kitchen, the soft rustle of coconut leaves overhead.

Rajiv opened the door before Mark could knock.

'Please come in, Doctor,' he said.

Inside, the living room was modest and neatly kept. A faded sofa set, a glass-topped centre table, framed devotional pictures on one wall and family photographs arranged carefully on another. There was nothing outwardly sinister about the place.

'This is Arati, my wife,' Rajiv said, gesturing towards a woman standing near the doorway to the kitchen.

She was young, perhaps twenty-five or twenty-six. Her hair was tied back hastily and her hands were still damp, as though she had just finished washing dishes.

'This is Dr Mark,' Rajiv continued. 'He is an expert in paranormal and supernatural activities. He is here to help us.'

Arati nodded, her expression a mixture of hope and unease.

Mark returned the nod politely and glanced around the room once more before speaking.

'Do you feel or see anything unusual here?' he asked her.

She hesitated, choosing her words carefully. 'I do not see the ghost,' she said. 'Only Unni sees it. Like in that film… The Sixth Sense. But sometimes…' She paused, lowering her voice. 'Sometimes I feel a negative energy. As if something heavy and cold passing by.'

Mark raised an eyebrow slightly.

'And there is more,' she added quickly. 'I sometimes find objects displaced. Things I am sure I kept in one place turn up somewhere else.'

Mark walked slowly around the room, his face carefully composed. He stopped near the corner where a small shelf held a brass lamp and a framed photograph of a deity.

'I can feel it,' he said slowly. 'There is indeed a strong negative presence here.'

Rajiv's breath caught. Arati clasped her hands together.

'There is a ghost in this house,' Mark said gravely.

He watched their faces closely as he spoke. Rajiv looked pale. Arati's eyes widened. Only Unni, seated cross-legged on the floor with a toy car, seemed oblivious to the tension thickening around him.

Mark crouched down in front of the boy.

'Unni,' he said gently, 'can you show me where you saw the ghost?'

The boy looked up, unfazed. 'Everywhere,' he said simply. 'Sometimes he has two red horns on his head. He also has a tail.'

Mark straightened abruptly, his eyes widening in exaggerated alarm.

'Oh my God,' he exclaimed. 'This may not be a ghost at all.'

Rajiv stiffened. 'What do you mean?'

Mark turned slowly towards them. 'This could be the devil.'

Arati let out a small gasp. Rajiv's face drained of colour.

'When did Unni first see this… being?' Mark asked.

Arati spoke after a pause. 'One night,' she said. 'Unni said he saw someone in the living room. I did not see anyone. Then he said the man was standing behind me. I turned around. There was nothing. He said the man walked away.'

Mark turned back to the child. 'Is that true, Unni?'

The boy answered at once. 'Yes. Amma cannot see him. I can.'

'Did he have horns and a tail then?' Mark asked.

Unni frowned, thinking hard. 'No. Not that time. He looked like a man. Later he had horns and tail.'

Mark stood up slowly and began to examine the walls. His gaze lingered on the framed photographs.

'Do you have your wedding album here?' he asked casually. 'I would like to see it.'

Rajiv hesitated for a second, then went into the bedroom and returned with a large album.

'Is this going to help?' he asked anxiously.

'Yes,' Mark replied. 'Negative entities often leave abstract imprints on photographs. Sometimes a ritual or an emotional event like a wedding can summon them.'

He flipped through the album slowly, occasionally pausing as though noticing something invisible to others.

'Why did you not leave this house and move back to your parents' place if you felt something was wrong?' Mark asked Arati.

'I do not think the house itself is haunted,' she said quickly. 'I feel the ghost is following Unni. Even if we move, it will follow us.'

Rajiv said quietly, 'I felt the same.'

Mark closed the album with a decisive snap.

'You are right,' he said. 'This is not tied to the house.'

Arati's eyes filled with tears. 'Then what is it?'

Mark walked towards the window and looked outside, pretending to assess something beyond the glass.

'Sometimes,' he said slowly, 'the devil uses children as mediums. He tries to communicate through them.'

Rajiv's voice trembled. 'Communicate what?'

Mark turned back sharply. 'Warnings. Threats. Messages.'

He looked down at Unni again. 'Did the devil say anything to you?'

The boy continued, unfazed. 'He said Dad is an idiot,' Unni said matter-of-factly. 'He said he will kill my dad.'

The room fell silent.

Arati covered her mouth with her hand. Rajiv staggered back and sank onto the sofa.

'This is serious,' Mark said quietly. 'Very serious.'

He straightened, his expression now firm and authoritative.

'I will need to assemble my equipment,' he said. 'I have specialised gadgets to deal with entities like this.'

Rajiv looked up at him with desperate hope. 'You can stop it?'

'I will try,' Mark said. 'But this requires careful planning. First, we need to know what the devil wants.'

He glanced at the calendar hanging on the wall. 'The energy around this place will peak during the temple festival. I will return on the evening of the festival.'

Arati spoke in a rush. 'We will do anything.'

Mark picked up his bag and headed towards the door.

'Do not perform any rituals until then,' he warned. 'And do not confront the entity on your own.'

Rajiv followed him to the door. 'Thank you, Doctor,' he said, his voice barely steady.

Mark stepped out into the fading daylight. As he walked back to his car, his face changed. The grave mask slipped, replaced by a sharp, thoughtful calm. He glanced back once at the house, then drove away.

*

The ancestral house stood wrapped in shadows and memory. That tharavadu's wooden pillars and walls absorbed the day's heat and released it into the cool air.

Mark sat alone in his room.

It was a small room. The ceiling was low and the tiled floor bore the faint scars of generations who had walked across it barefoot. The old chair creaked softly under his weight as he reclined as he stared at nothing and everything at once.

Rajiv's face came to him first. The tightness around his

eyes. The way his fingers kept rubbing against each other when he spoke. Then Arati, her careful pauses, the practiced calm that barely concealed fear. And Unni. The child's unblinking certainty, the casual way he spoke of horns and tails, as though describing a neighbour he saw every day.

Mark replayed every gesture in his mind. The father's protective urgency. The mother's quiet dread. The boy's vivid imagination or perhaps something else entirely. He ran through the scene again and again, stripping it down to its smallest details, searching for fractures where truth might slip through.

Sometimes, despite being trained as a psychiatrist, Mark found himself stepping back into the tools of psychology. Observation. Behavioural cues. The subtle contagion of fear. He wondered if this was one of those cases where belief itself became the illness.

He leaned forward and rested his elbows on his knees, his fingers interlocked.

Fear, he knew, could shape reality. Especially in a child. Especially in a house where silence had too much room to grow.

His eyes drifted to the photograph on the table beside him.

It was an old frame, its edges worn smooth. Inside it was a picture taken ten years ago. Mark and Saranya stood close together, smiling awkwardly at the camera, caught between shyness and happiness. She wore a pale blue sari. His arm rested lightly on her shoulder.

Mark stared at the photograph.

At first, it was just a photograph. Then something in his chest loosened.

His gaze softened. His breathing slowed. The sounds of the tharavadu faded, replaced by a different world.

He was back at the Medical College.

The corridors were crowded and noisy. He saw himself younger, thinner, walking with hurried confidence. And then he saw her.

Saranya stood near the notice board, struggling to pin up a paper that refused to stay put. She was a junior. He remembered noticing her not because of beauty alone, but because of her laugh. It had been unguarded, ringing, completely out of place in a building obsessed with discipline and suffering.

Their conversations replayed themselves. Tea breaks stretched longer than they should have. Shared notes. Arguments over diagnoses. Long walks after lectures, pretending they had nowhere else to be.

The years after college unfolded like a gentle montage. Distance. Phone calls late into the night. The certainty that grew slowly, stubbornly. Marriage at thirty. The quiet pride of building a life that finally felt complete.

For a moment, Mark smiled.

Then the light dimmed.

The images blurred, as though someone had smeared the edges of memory with ash. A scream tore through the silence.

Saranya's voice.

Pain-filled. Raw.

Mark's chest tightened. He heard the rapid beeping of monitors. The clatter of metal trays. The sharp commands of doctors cutting through chaos. The smell of disinfectant grew overpowering, mixed with something darker.

He tried to move, but his body would not obey.

Then came the cry of a baby. Thin. Fragile. Alive.

For a second, hope flared.

And then everything collapsed.

The scene shifted violently.

Fire roared. Flames licked at wood and cloth. Saranya's body lay still, wrapped in white, the contours of her face already slipping away from the world. Smoke stung his eyes. His throat burned. His knees gave way.

Mark sobbed.

The sound came from deep within him, tearing its way out without permission.

A hand gripped his shoulder.

'Hey. What happened?'

The voice pulled him back, hard and sudden.

Mark gasped and blinked rapidly. The room returned in fragments. The old chair. The dim lamp. Viswamitran standing beside him, worry etched across his face.

'I heard you crying,' Viswamitran said softly.

It took Mark a few seconds to anchor himself fully in the present.

'Oh,' he said finally. 'It is those visions again.'

Viswamitran pulled another chair and sat opposite him. 'Why don't you treat yourself? You know more than anyone else. Surely there is some treatment.'

Mark looked at the photograph again.

'There are ways,' he said quietly. 'Medication. Therapy. Techniques to shut it down.'

'Then why don't you?'

Mark's fingers traced the edge of the frame.

'I do not know,' he admitted. 'No matter how painful it is, there is a strange comfort in it. Seeing her again. Feeling her presence. It is like a lucid dream. I am aware it is not real, but it feels… close.'

Viswamitran sighed. 'You are punishing yourself.'

'Maybe,' Mark said. 'Or maybe this is the only way I still get to be with her.'

There was a long silence between them.

Finally, Viswamitran stood up. 'You know yourself better than anyone else, brother. Dinner is ready. Come.'

Mark nodded slowly. He placed the photograph face down on the table and rose from the chair.

*

Mark needed gadgets for his ghost hunting at Rajiv's house, but his real instruments lay far away in Thiruvananthapuram. Carbon monoxide detectors, infrared cameras, portable oxygen analysers, all of it useless to him now because distance mattered. The tharavadu offered none of these comforts. What it did offer was silence, darkness and time.

That night, while the rest of the ancestral house slept, Mark worked alone in his room. On the table lay a strange assortment of objects that would have baffled anyone else. A roll of duct tape. A half-crushed tube of superglue. A hand drill borrowed from the caretaker's shed. Screws taken from a broken cupboard hinge. A scratched analogue metre salvaged from a discarded voltage stabiliser.

Mark sat cross-legged on the floor, sweat beading at his temples. He worked slowly, methodically. He drilled holes into a cheap plastic casing with precise and surgical movements. He connected wires that led nowhere, taped them with exaggerated care and glued the casing shut with a firmness that suggested permanence. When he tapped the metre, the needle jumped and settled back slightly off zero.

Perfect.

He lifted the device, weighed it in his palm and turned it this way and that under the lamp. It looked serious. Heavy. Dangerous. The kind of object people instinctively feared and trusted at the same time.

The next evening, Mark arrived at Rajiv's house. The village had already begun transforming itself for the temple festival. Chenda drums rolled continuously, deep and primal, vibrating through the earth. Strings of coloured bulbs hung from electric poles, flickering unevenly, casting strange shadows on the road.

Rajiv opened the door almost immediately.

'Doctor, we were expecting you,' he said, relief flooding his face.

Inside, the house smelled of freshly lit incense and coconut oil. Arati stood near the bedroom doorway, dressed in a cream and gold kasavu saree, her hair neatly braided, jasmine flowers tucked in with care. The effort could not hide the tension in her eyes. Unni stood close to her leg, fingers gripping the fabric of her saree.

Mark stepped inside slowly.

He paused near the centre of the room. He closed his eyes. He stretched his arms outward, palms facing down, fingers slightly curled. He breathed in deeply, then exhaled through his mouth, as though tasting the air.

'It is strong tonight,' Mark said softly. 'Much stronger than before.'

Rajiv stiffened.

'Tonight, the devil will communicate with us,' Mark continued, opening his eyes. 'For that, I need your family photograph.'

Rajiv hurried to the shelf and returned with a framed photograph of the three of them. Their smiles were stiff, their posture formal, the kind of photograph taken more for record than memory. Mark accepted it with both hands and placed it carefully on the centre table. From his bag, he removed a folded black cloth and lay it on front of the photograph.

From a small pouch, he poured a thin circle of salt on the black cloth. His fingers moved with ritualistic slowness. He then sprinkled turmeric powder inside the circle. Finally, he pinched *kunkum* between his fingers and traced crude symbols across the floor, red lines cutting through yellow and white.

The sigil looked chaotic, violent and unsettling.

Mark rose and reached into his bag. He brought out the black gadget he had built the previous night. The needle trembled faintly as he placed it near the photograph.

'This is an EMF metre,' Mark said gravely. 'It detects electromagnetic disturbances. Ordinary cameras cannot capture entities like this. But negative energies distort invisible fields. When the devil moves, this needle will react. It doesn't record any image or video like a camera. It just senses the variations in invisible energy.'

Rajiv stared at the device as though it might explode.

'What is the purpose of the sigil?' he asked.

Mark turned slowly.

'Listen carefully,' he said. 'Tonight, none of you must stay in this house.'

Rajiv stiffened. 'What do you mean?'

'Go to any relative's house. Attend the festival. This is an auspicious night,' Mark said. 'When the house is empty, the devil will feel free to reveal himself. He will destroy the sigil. He cannot tolerate it.'

Arati's voice trembled. 'And the photograph?'

Mark looked at the frame.

'When we return tomorrow, the devil will have left a mark on one person in the photograph. That mark tells us whom he wants gone.'

Rajiv frowned. 'Gone how?'

Mark met his eyes without blinking.

'If Arati is marked, she must leave the family. If Unni is marked, you must send him away. An orphanage, if necessary. For his safety. If you are marked, Rajiv, then you must stay away from this house and leave the mother and child behind.'

The words fell like stones.

'Is this the only way?' Rajiv asked, his voice barely a whisper.

'Let us see what the devil wants,' he said calmly. 'Only then can we negotiate.'

He walked around the room, scanning corners, ceiling beams, the narrow hallway leading to the bedrooms.

'Remove all images of deities,' he said suddenly. 'The devil needs freedom to express himself.'

Rajiv hesitated, then began lifting framed gods from shelves. Arati followed, wrapping brass idols in cloth with trembling hands. Ganesha, Krishna, Durga, all disappeared into cupboards and bags. The familiar guardians of the house were stripped away one by one.

The house felt hollow.

They locked the doors carefully. Rajiv checked the latch twice.

Outside, the festival had reached a fever pitch. Drums thundered, drowning out thought.

They walked away together, blending into the crowd heading towards the temple. Arati turned back once, her eyes lingering on the darkened house.

The temple festival unfolded that night like a living river of sound and light. Mark walked beside Viswamitran and his family through the packed temple grounds. Rows of oil lamps burned along the outer wall, their flames trembling in the night breeze, turning the stone corridors into rivers of gold. The chenda melam rose and fell in powerful waves. Drums spoke language older than words, vibrating deep inside the chest.

Viswamitran's children darted ahead, momentarily freed from their phones by the spectacle. They stared wide-eyed at the towering decorated lamps, the vendors shouting over one another, selling sugarcane juice, balloons and fried bananas. Sulekha stood close to Mark, pointing out familiar faces, exchanging nods and half-smiles with neighbours and relatives. Mark watched the procession with quiet interest, noting how ritual, rhythm and collective belief fused people into a single organism for a few hours.

The caparisoned deity emerged from the sanctum, borne on shoulders, surrounded by flickering torches. Conch shells were blown. Mark folded his hands, not in prayer, but in respect for the human need for meaning and spectacle. He spoke little, content to observe, to blend into the flow.

Elsewhere in the same crowd, Rajiv moved like a man walking underwater. The drums unsettled him. His eyes kept drifting towards the dark road that led back to his house. The image of the sigil and the photograph gnawed at his mind. He barely noticed Unni tugging at his hand or Arati speaking to him. Rajiv felt only dread. Every chant sounded like a warning. Every shadow felt like a countdown. The celebration surged on around him, but his thoughts remained locked inside that silent house, waiting for the devil to choose.

Rajiv and his family spent the night at a friend's house, but sleep never truly came to them. He lay awake on the thin mattress, staring into the darkness, imagining the house he had locked behind him. Somewhere inside it, according to Dr Mark, something waited. Arati slept in short, restless bursts, waking often to check on Unni, who murmured in his sleep.

At dawn, they returned.

Dr Mark was already there.

He stood near the gate, hands in his pockets, his posture relaxed.

'Doctor, you're already here,' Rajiv asked.

'Yes,' Mark replied evenly. 'These things needn't wait.'

Rajiv gave a short breath and unlocked the door. The latch clicked open with a sound that seemed too loud in the still morning. Arati hesitated, then stepped inside, holding Unni close.

The house greeted them with silence.

Rajiv's eyes went immediately to the table.

The sigil was destroyed.

What had been carefully arranged the previous evening now lay in chaos. The neat circles of salt were smeared into uneven streaks. Turmeric was scattered across. Kunkum had been pressed and dragged, leaving rough red marks. The black cloth lay twisted to one side, singed at the edges.

Arati gasped and clutched her chest.

Rajiv staggered forward, his knees weakening.

'The devil was here,' he exclaimed, horror cracking his voice. 'It came. It really came.'

Mark remained silent, watching.

Then Rajiv saw the photograph.

The framed family picture lay on its back. Rajiv's own face had been marked heavily with a thick stain of kunkum, turmeric and salt. The pigments blurred his eyes and mouth, pressing him into the image like a verdict.

Arati let out a small cry.

'What does this mean?' she asked.

Mark turned slowly to Rajiv. His gaze was steady.

Rajiv collapsed onto a chair, his body giving up all resistance.

'For the safety of my wife and son, I will leave,' he said through tears. 'I will go away. If that is what it wants, I will go.'

Arati knelt beside him, holding his shoulders.

'Wait,' Mark said calmly. 'I am taking this EMF metre with me. I need to examine it carefully. If the entity demanded anything more, it will be reflected in the readings. I will call you after that. Then we will decide the next step. Do not panic.'

Rajiv looked up, clinging to the certainty in Mark's voice.

Mark picked up the black device from the table, slipped it into his bag, and walked out of the house without another glance at the ruined sigil.

The door closed softly behind him.

Rajiv broke down.

The tharavadu was cool and dim when Mark returned. He went straight to his room, closed the door and opened his laptop on the old wooden desk. Mark connected the device and accessed the stored data.

The footage loaded.

He watched it once, his face unreadable. He watched it again, more slowly. His lips pressed into a thin line.

His suspicions were confirmed.

A strange mix of relief and sadness settled in his chest. Relief that his reasoning had been correct. Sadness because the truth was uglier than any imagined demon. For a fleeting moment, he thought it would have been easier if there truly had been a devil.

He picked up his phone and called Rajiv.

'Come to the tharavadu,' Mark said. 'Come alone.'

Rajiv arrived an hour later. Mark led him into the room and shut the door. The ceiling fan turned slowly above them.

Mark opened the laptop and turned it towards Rajiv.

'Rajiv,' he said, his voice low but firm. 'I have to tell you something openly.'

He paused at the threshold, steadying himself.

'I do not believe in ghosts or devils or demons,' Mark continued. 'I am completely certain of that. That certainty is what made me suspicious from the moment you told me your story. The signs were obvious. But belief blinded you.'

Rajiv frowned weakly.

'Belief in ghosts?' he asked.

Mark shook his head.

'No,' he said quietly. 'Belief in your wife.'

Mark looked at Rajiv, as though weighing how much truth a man could bear in a single sitting.

'Now I have to tell you the truth,' Mark said quietly. 'I lied.'

Rajiv stiffened. His fingers tightened around the arms of the chair.

'That machine I called an EMF metre,' Mark continued, lifting the black gadget from the table, 'it is nothing of the sort. I assembled it from scrap parts I found here and there. Old casings, a discarded metre needle, wires that aren't connected to anything. Inside it, I placed a small infrared pen camera which I usually carry with me all the time. The body hides it well, but the lens faces straight ahead. It recorded everything that happened in your house last night.'

Rajiv stared at the device as though it might leap up and confess on its own.

'I retrieved the footage,' Mark said. 'Now I will show you something.'

He opened the laptop again and pressed play.

The screen flickered to life.

Rajiv recognised his living room instantly. The angle was fixed, slightly tilted, showing the main door, the table, the framed photograph and the the sigil. The image was in black and white but clear enough. Time passed silently. Nothing moved.

Then the door opened.

Rajiv inched closer and focused his eyes.

A man stepped inside.

Not a shadow. Not a shape. A man. Flesh and bone. He moved with familiarity, shutting the door behind him, glancing around as if he knew the house well. He walked to the table, bent down and deliberately dragged his fingers through the salt and powders. He pressed pigments onto Rajiv's face in the photograph with careful precision, wiped his hands on the cloth and left.

The door closed.

The video ended.

The room felt suddenly airless.

'Do you know this man?' Mark asked softly.

Rajiv could not answer at once. His mouth opened but no sound came. His eyes remained fixed on the frozen frame, as though the image might change if he stared long enough. It felt as if he had just watched the devil unmask himself.

'Yes,' Rajiv finally whispered. His voice cracked. 'I know him.'

Mark nodded.

'It is Arati's friend,' Rajiv said, disbelief flooding his words. 'Why is he in my house?'

Mark drew back, folding his arms.

'You are still blinded by the trust you place in your wife,' he said. 'Listen carefully. I will explain everything.'

Rajiv lowered his head, his shoulders slumping.

'When I first came to your house,' Mark continued, 'every time I spoke about ghosts or devils, I watched Arati's face. She tried too hard to agree with me. Fear looks different. Belief looks different. What I saw was confirmation. She wanted the story to be true.'

Rajiv looked away.

'Then I looked at your wedding album,' Mark said. 'You did not notice it because you were looking at your own happiness. But she looked detached. Her smile never reached her eyes. She was present in the ceremony, not in the marriage.'

Rajiv closed his eyes.

'Then Unni spoke,' Mark said. 'He said the man did not

have horns or a tail the first time he saw him. That detail was the crack. From that moment, I was certain.'

Rajiv looked up slowly.

'This is what happened,' Mark said. 'You were away, working in another country. During that time, Arati's male friend began visiting her for whatever reasons, frequently. At first, Unni was too small to understand.'

Mark paused, choosing his words.

'One day, he noticed properly. He called out to his mother and said there was a man standing there. A stranger. That was when she invented the story. She said she could not see anyone. The man understood immediately and played along. From then on, whenever he came and Unni saw him, both of them pretended he did not exist.'

Rajiv's hands trembled.

'Children trust their parents more than their eyes,' Mark said. 'Confusion grows easily in such soil. And slowly, the story changed. The man became something else. Something frightening. Something that could not be questioned.'

Rajiv felt his chest tighten.

'The insults came next,' Mark added. 'Subtle ones. The man mocking you in front of your son. Planting ideas. Twisting the child's fear into certainty.'

Mark waited until Rajiv had settled into the chair again. The man looked smaller now, as if the truth had physically reduced him.

'Rajiv,' he said, 'what your wife did to your son has a name. It is called gaslighting.'

Rajiv frowned. 'Gaslighting?'

'Yes,' Mark said. 'It is a form of psychological manipulation. The aim is simple but cruel. You make another person doubt their own perception, memory and sanity. You tell them what they saw is not real. What they felt is wrong. Over time, they stop trusting their own senses.'

Rajiv's jaw tightened.

'The term comes from a British play from the 1930s, later adapted into a film called Gaslight,' Mark continued. 'In the story, a husband slowly drives his wife to the edge of madness. He dims the gas lamps in their house, just a little. When she notices and asks about it, he tells her nothing has changed. He hides objects and then accuses her of misplacing them. Every time she questions reality, he calmly denies it. Eventually, she begins to believe that she is losing her mind.'

Mark closed in.

'That is gaslighting. Not shouting. Not violence. Quiet denial. Repeated insistence that the victim is wrong.'

Rajiv stared at the floor.

'Now think about Unni,' Mark continued. 'A child sees a man in his house. He does the most natural thing. He calls his mother. She looks at the same place and says she sees nothing. She tells him there is no one there.'

Rajiv closed his eyes.

'The child trusts his mother more than his own eyes,' Mark went on. 'So when she says the man is not real, the child assumes the fault lies in him. His mind searches for another explanation. That is where fear enters.'

Mark paused, letting the words settle.

'The man continues to appear. Each time, your wife repeats the same denial. Soon the child stops saying "there is a man" and starts asking "why am I seeing him". To make sense of this contradiction, the mind creates a story. A ghost. A devil. Something invisible to adults.'

Rajiv's breathing grew uneven.

'Once that story is planted,' Mark said, 'it becomes easy to shape it. Add horns. Add a tail. Add menace. The child is already primed to believe that his reality is unreliable. Fear fills the gaps.'

He straightened in his chair.

'Wha…what about the horns and the tail?' Rajiv asked hoarsely.

Mark sighed.

'You can buy devil horns in any toy shop,' he said. 'A tail can be made from a rope or cloth. Cheap theatrics. Enough to frighten a child. Enough to convince an adult who already believes.'

Rajiv shook his head slowly.

'And last evening,' Mark continued, 'everything I did with the sigil, the markings, the rules, it was a trap. Your wife knew the story had to continue. She needed you away. She needed the devil to confirm itself.'

Mark tapped the laptop lightly.

'She must have called her friend as soon as you left. He would already have a copy of the house key. He came in, destroyed the sigil, marked the photograph and left. A perfect performance. Just to make their story convincing. Just to confirm a nonsense that I presented there.'

The room fell into silence.

Rajiv sat unmoving. His face had gone pale. His eyes were hollow, staring at nothing.

'Blind belief is dangerous,' Mark said quietly. 'Belief in religion, belief in ghosts or belief in a person you love. Any belief that refuses to question can ruin you.'

Tears slipped down Rajiv's cheeks. He did not wipe them away.

'What should I do now?' he asked with a defeated voice.

Mark softened his tone.

'My job here is done,' he said. 'I came to prove that there are no ghosts or demons in your house. What you do next is your choice.'

He reached into his bag and handed Rajiv a pen drive.

'This footage can be given to your lawyer,' Mark said. 'You should also consider a paternity test for Unni. Whatever you decide, do not confront or attack Arati. Do not raise your hand or your voice. The law will not be on your side. If you act rashly, you will destroy yourself and make things easier for her.'

Rajiv nodded slowly.

'Collect evidence,' Mark continued. 'Speak to a lawyer. Proceed carefully. Or you can choose to ignore all this and continue living in comfort built on lies. The choice is yours.'

Rajiv stood up, unsteady. He took the pen drive with trembling fingers.

'Thank you,' he said, bowing his head slightly.

He turned and walked out of the room.

Mark closed the laptop and sat alone for a moment, listening to the distant sounds of the house.

His phone rang.

Viswamitran's name flashed on the screen.

'Come,' Viswamitran said cheerfully. 'The second night of the festival has begun.'

Mark stood, straightened his shirt and stepped out into the fading light, leaving behind one truth revealed and another celebration waiting.

CHAPTER SIX

Anomaly

Dr Mark kept a structured rhythm to his life. His home, designed in unmistakable tropical-modern style, doubled as his private clinic on select days. Mark consulted at home only on Mondays, Tuesdays and Saturdays. On Wednesdays and Thursdays, he travelled to Satyananda Memorial Hospital, an hour away, for consultations there. Fridays and Sundays were sacred, time for experiments in his small home laboratory, tinkering with computers and chemical setups or indulging in painting and writing.

He had published a bestselling self-help book, though he never spoke of it unless asked. He stayed away from social media entirely. His view was simple: Human evolution hasn't caught up with the dopamine assault of endless scrolling. He preferred quiet, books and controlled curiosity.

Ashok, ever dutiful, managed the waiting area. He sat behind a wooden desk just outside Mark's consultation room, calling out names from the appointment list, collecting fees and ensuring order in the calm space. The waiting chairs lined the wall beneath soft yellow wall lamps.

That Monday evening, the last of the scheduled patients had already left. The air inside felt cooler, quieter, the kind of silence that comes after a long day of listening, diagnosing, reassuring.

But one woman remained seated.

She looked out of place among the cushions and the soft lighting. She seemed to be in her late-twenties, hair tied in a hurried knot, no jewellery, clothes slightly wrinkled, exhaustion etched into the corners of her eyes. She sat with her hands clasped tightly.

Ashok stepped toward her, puzzled.

'Madam… you didn't take an appointment?' he asked gently.

She looked up. Her eyes were red, tired.

'Is that necessary?' she asked, voice soft, almost apologetic. 'I didn't know.'

'Yes, usually you need an appointment to meet the doctor,' Ashok explained.

'It's not about any illness,' she said quickly, shaking her head. 'I… I just want to talk to him. To tell him that something he said on TV is wrong.'

Ashok blinked. That was not the usual reason people came here.

'Wrong?' he repeated, unsure.

'Please,' she whispered. 'Just ask him if he can spare a moment. I only want to talk.'

'Alright,' he said finally. 'Wait here.'

He slipped into Mark's consulting room, closing the door softly behind him.

Mark looked up from his notes. Ashok told him about the strange encounter outside.

Mark told Ashok to let the lady in. Maybe it'll take five

more minutes of his time. He didn't bother. The woman entered the room slowly, bracing herself as though about to reveal a terrible burden.

Mark reclined slightly in his chair with sharpened curiosity.

'Yes, tell me,' he said politely. 'What's your name and where are you from?'

'I'm Stella,' she said. 'From Jainagar Colony.'

Jainagar Colony - the polite, modern label given by the City Council. In reality, it was the state's largest slum, a place with a heavier, older name the officials preferred to forget.

He knew its history well.

For generations, oppressed castes had lived there in cramped huts and shacks, clustered under rusted tin roofs. Thirty years ago, the government built squat, concrete apartment blocks, two to three floors each and relocated the residents, calling it "urban renewal."

But the scars of the past still lingered in the alleyways.

Once, many surviving on petty crime or serving as hired hands for local gangs. Now, most had shifted to honest work as garage owners, scrap dealers, recyclers, mechanics.

And then there was the conversion. A fringe European missionary sect had swept through six decades back, promising scholarships, rice bags and salvation to a community beaten down by caste and poverty. Thousands converted. Thousands stayed inside the colony, rarely stepping beyond its borders except for work as housemaids, electricians or casual labourers.

A world within a world.

Mark knew all of this - the sociology, the psychology, the generational trauma.

Yet he had never expected someone from Jainagar to walk into his consultation room. And certainly not someone who wanted to argue with him.

'What seems to be the problem, Ms Stella?' Mark asked,

folding his hands.

Stella's tired eyes hardened with a conviction that surprised him.

'I saw your video online,' she said. 'You said there's no such thing as curses. No paranormal forces.'

'Yes,' Mark replied calmly. 'Everything has a scientific explanation. Rational, observable, testable. That's what I meant.'

'I came here to tell you that you're wrong,' Stella said, leaning forward. Her voice no longer trembled. It was resolute. 'I have seen the cursed object myself. And I…and others in my colony…are suffering because of it.'

For the first time, Mark's expression shifted.

Not fear. Not belief. But interest.

The kind of spark that lit his mind whenever someone presented a fresh myth begging to be debunked.

He lifted his eyebrows slightly.

'Please… tell me everything,' Mark said, leaning forward. 'And I'll show you the rational explanation behind it. Whatever this object is, it isn't cursed. Most likely it's something ordinary, made frightening by coincidences and collective imagination.'

'You know, Doctor… you really are arrogant,' Stella said. 'If it weren't for the trouble that cursed object is causing in my colony, I wouldn't be here. I only wanted to show you that you don't always have the answers.'

Mark's lips twitched into a small, amused smile.

'Alright, Stella,' he said softly. 'Tell me everything about this cursed object. Start from the beginning.'

He brought himself forward, elbows resting on the table. Stella clasped her hands together.

'It started last month,' she said in a low voice. 'Some scrap collectors from our colony brought in what they thought was a thermos flask, something they'd scavenged from the city.

But they kept saying it didn't feel like one. The metal was too heavy… too warm… and the casing didn't look like anything they'd seen before.'

She looked at Mark, searching for a trace of disbelief in his eyes. She found none, only that clinical, unsettling calm he carried everywhere.

'Titus, who has a scrap shop, bought it,' she continued. 'Gave them a thousand rupees on the spot. He never pays that much unless he's absolutely sure it's valuable.'

Her gaze drifted, as if transported back into the noise and dust of the colony's metal yard. Titus and Dony inside the scrap shop.

The tube light above them buzzed and flickered which was throwing jittery shadows across the cluttered scrap shop. Metal scraps clanged softly as rats scurried somewhere deep in the piles. In the middle of the chaos, Titus and Dony stood hunched over the strange, heavy cylinder that sat on their workbench like an uninvited guest.

Dony, Titus's assistant, who is just 20 years old, poked it with a screwdriver, his face twisted with doubt.

'Titus bro… I'm telling you, they cheated you,' he muttered. 'This thing looks like some duplicate nonsense.'

Titus straightened slowly as his broad shoulders tightened under his faded shirt. He was a man who clawed through three decades of junk and still trusted his instincts more than any machine.

'Kid,' he said, tapping the object with his knuckles. The sound was unsettling, solid, dense, almost too deep. 'I've been in this business for thirty years. Aluminium doesn't sound like this. Steel doesn't feel like this. Whatever this is… we've never handled anything like it before.'

He ran his calloused fingers along the smooth metallic surface, tracing the patterns etched into it, symbols that looked neither written nor welded, more like something grown into the metal.

'There's something inside,' Titus continued. 'And even the outer casing will fetch a price.'

Dony shifted, biting his lip. 'I still don't trust Joy and Mebin. They're not scrap collectors, Titus bro… they're thieves. They steal from places they shouldn't even walk near.'

'Exactly,' Titus said with eyes glittered with excitement. 'That's why I bought this. Whatever they stole… it wasn't from any ordinary goddamn place.'

They spent the next hour examining it, turning it, shaking it, holding it up to the light. No seam. No latch. No hinge. Only those eerie markings and a seamless cylinder that defied every tool they brought to it.

Hammers bounced off.

Crowbars slipped.

Not a single dent.

It was as if the thing refused to be opened.

Finally, breathing heavily and defeated, Titus wiped his forehead with a dirty cloth.

'Forget it for now,' he grumbled. 'Leave it in the corner. We've got real work to do. We'll try again when we're free.'

Dony hauled the object to a shadowy corner, the metal thudding against the dusty floor. It sat there silently like something waiting.

Over the next few days, Titus couldn't help himself. Every customer, every passerby, even children who wandered too close were pulled toward the corner.

'Come here, look at this,' he'd call, with a mixture of pride and unease.

People examined it with puzzled frowns.

'A thermos flask?'

'Part of a train engine?'

'Some military gadget?'

'Rocket launcher piece?'

'Alien artefact, bro!'

Titus inched closer, squinting at the strange markings etched into the metal. Under the flickering tube light, the patterns shimmered faintly.

'Oh... Jesus,' he whispered, more to himself than to Dony. For the first time, Titus sounded unsure. Dony stood beside him, arms crossed uneasily. His eyes darted between the object and the shadows gathering in the corners of the shop.

'Titus bro... look at those symbols,' he murmured. 'That doesn't look like anything human-made. What if... what if it's some alien artefact?'

Titus shot him a sharp glance.

'Alien...?' he scoffed. 'Maybe it is...?'

He tapped one of the markings again. It gave off no echo, no vibration, nothing. Almost like the metal swallowed the sound.

'Still,' he muttered, 'this isn't something ordinary.'

A thought struck him, and he straightened abruptly.

'How did Joy and Mebin get this? Those two don't usually stumble upon such artefacts.'

Dony scratched the back of his neck, hesitant. 'I think you should ask them. They must've lifted it from somewhere important.'

'They'll never say,' Titus sighed, shaking his head. 'Those boys keep their mouths shut tighter than this damned cylinder. They've never told me their sources before. Why would they start now?'

Dony nudged him with an elbow, trying to sound braver than he felt.

'Still... just ask, man. What's the harm? Maybe this time

they'll talk.'

Titus stared at the object again. Something about its warm, smooth surface made the hairs on the back of his neck rise.

'Yeah,' he said quietly. 'Maybe I should.'

The decision to go find Joy and Mebin gnawed at Titus long after Dony fell silent. The strange cylinder still sat in the corner of the scrap shop. He tried to shake off the unease, muttered a curse under his breath and kicked his old motorcycle to life.

The engine sputtered reluctantly and echoed across the rusty, dirty street of the colony.

The ride to the far edge of the colony was barely twenty minutes, but the path felt longer than usual. The evening light was fading, turning the cramped lanes of Jainagar Colony into darker, narrower veins. Children who normally played cricket in the dust were nowhere to be seen. The neighbourhood dogs barked with some difficulty.

When Titus turned the final corner toward Joy's house, he felt his stomach twist. A crowd had gathered, murmuring, whispering, some crying, some simply staring in stunned silence. No one laughed. Few people were smoking outside. Most of them were standing stiff with their faces drained of colour.

Titus parked the bike and pushed through the wall of bodies.

'What happened?' he asked, tapping the shoulder of a man standing near the doorway.

The man turned, his eyes red-rimmed.

'Joy died,' he said flatly. 'And… Mebin too.'

Titus blinked. This was unexpected.

'What? Both? How? They were fine the last time I saw!'

The man shook his head, rubbing his face as if trying to make sense of it himself.

'No idea. They were healthy. Then suddenly diarrhoea, terrible headaches… and…' He hesitated, swallowing hard. 'Their hands started decaying. Skin peeling. Fingers blackening. Like something was eating them from inside.'

A cold shiver crawled down Titus's spine.

'Didn't they see a doctor?' he whispered.

The man scoffed bitterly. 'Here? You know how it is. First, they went for prayer service. Pastor Isaac said it was an "attack of evil". A test of faith. By the time the local clinic doctor saw them, he said food poisoning. But Joy kept getting worse. Mebin too.' He lowered his voice. 'Big hospitals… we don't trust them. They take money and give nothing. If God can't cure, then maybe… it was their time.'

Titus felt the ground vibrate beneath him.

He didn't say another word. He simply moved past the man and stepped inside.

The air inside was cries, sweat and the grief of too many people packed into too small a space. Joy's mother sat in a corner, wailing softly, rocking back and forth.

Titus approached slowly.

When he saw Joy's corpse, he felt as if gripped by coldness.

It wasn't the peaceful stillness he expected. Joy's skin was mottled with strange sores, his fingertips darkened and decayed. His face was drawn tight as if frozen mid-scream. There was something disturbingly wrong as though death had been too slow, too painful and too unnatural.

Titus staggered back.

Night had already settled over Jainagar Colony by the time Titus rode back. The roads were quieter than usual, shadows thick under the streetlamps, the murmur of grief still echoing in his ears. Joy's lifeless face, the decay, the darkness in the fingertips, flashed before him again and again.

By the time he reached the scrap shop, the metal shutters

clinked softly in the evening breeze. He expected silence. Instead, he heard frantic footsteps inside… and a voice overflowing with excitement.

'Titus bro!' Dony burst out from behind a stack of rusted compressors. His grin stretched from ear to ear, his eyes gleaming with a boyish triumph. 'I opened it! I opened the canister!'

Titus froze in the doorway, helmet still in hand. Happiness and horror tangled inside him like barbed wire. He couldn't decide what his face was supposed to express.

'Open…?' Titus murmured, still half-lost in the news he carried. 'Dony, listen, Joy and Mebin…'

'Forget that, man!' Dony interrupted, bouncing on his feet. 'Come and see! You won't believe what was inside!'

Titus grabbed Dony's arm.

'Joy and Mebin are dead,' he said, his voice thin and hollow. 'Both of them. Something unnatural… something terrible happened.'

Dony's grin collapsed instantly.

'What?' he whispered. 'Dead? Both…?'

'Yes,' Titus said, rubbing a hand across his tired face. 'Something must've happened to them before they sold us that thing.'

Then, too suddenly, Dony blinked and a strange excitement resurfaced, pushing aside the shock like a child brushing away cobwebs.

'Anyways,' he whispered, tugging his sleeve. 'Just… just come look.'

Before Titus could respond, Dony lunged toward the wall and switched off the shop's interior light. The shop plunged into darkness. For a heartbeat, Titus's breath caught, until he saw it.

In the far corner of the room, a faint blue glow pulsed

softly, as if something was breathing in the dark.

Titus felt his skin crawl.

'What… is that?' he whispered.

'Look!' Dony scrambled ahead, nearly tripping over a pile of copper wires. 'When I cracked the canister with the chisels and hammer, this stuff poured out. Like salt… but not salt. And look…it glows in the dark. Titus bro! This is… this is something from another world!'

The eerie blue light glowed like faint heartbeat. Titus approached slowly.

Dony had placed the substance on a dented plastic plate. Up close, it looked like powdered salt, almost beautiful, yet it emitted a faint, acrid smell that stung the back of Titus's throat.

'What would it be?' Dony asked, whispering like they were standing over a forbidden treasure.

'I… I don't know,' Titus admitted. And for the first time in years, the man who thought he'd seen everything in the scrap world felt very, very small.

'But look at it, bro,' Dony breathed, mesmerised. 'It's… amazing.'

'It is,' Titus said reluctantly. 'But… I don't think we should sell it. Not to anyone. This is something special.'

'I'm telling you, bro… this thing is magical,' Dony whispered. 'Just watch.'

He pulled out his phone, opened the camera and pointed it toward the glowing salt. The moment the lens focused on the salt mound, the screen began to distort. Electronic grains crawled across it like insects under the glass. The image warped, colours bled and the camera struggled to lock focus. Within seconds, the display turned into a jittering grey fog.

Dony tapped the screen, tried again.

Nothing. Just grain and blur, as if the phone was refusing

to look at the substance.

He turned to Titus, almost breathless.

'See? It doesn't even allow itself to be photographed. Tell me that isn't magic.'

Dony's excitement flared again.

'Can I have some? Just a little? Please, bro… just a pinch.'

Titus hesitated. The glowing substance cast a ghostly shimmer across Dony's eager face. For a moment, Titus considered refusing. But exhaustion… confusion… and a strange, fatalistic shrug overcame him.

'…Fine,' he said quietly. 'Take some.'

Dony grinned, scooped a pinch into a handkerchief, folded it carefully into a piece of old newspaper, and tucked it into his jeans pocket like it was treasure stolen from heaven.

'I'll see you in the morning!' he said and rushed out.

Titus didn't take the glowing substance home that night. He left it on the plastic plate in the corner of the scrap shop. It looked like a relic from another age, or another world as though a prized possession meant for a museum. He locked the shop carefully and walked home through the narrow lanes

He told his wife about the substance and she expressed her wish to see it the next day.

Meanwhile, in Dony's house…

Dony, unlike Titus, had carried his tiny packet of the glowing salt home with the pride of a child bringing treasure. His house, one cramped room with an asbestos roof and a wooden cot, lit up with excitement the moment he showed the crystalline substance to his parents.

From that moment, the tiny home became a pilgrimage spot for gossiping neighbours.

'Dony, show us the magic thing…'

'What is this? Some kind of gemstone?'

'Keep it safe! It might be holy! Or… cursed…'

Dony basked in the attention.

At the same time, Titus's scrap shop wasn't much different. The glowing substance became a spectacle. Every passerby in the colony found an excuse to step inside.

'Titus bro, show us the light thing…'

'What if this is from space?'

'Call the pastor, man! Call him!'

Hundreds of hands waved above it and dozens of eyes stared at it in wonder.

Two days later…

Stella arrived at her parents' home just before dusk. Her six-year-old daughter, Lucy, clung to her hand, skipping along the narrow lane. Lucy's father was away in Tamil Nadu for electrical contract work, leaving Stella and Lucy alone most weeks.

Dony was waiting at the door, practically vibrating with excitement.

'Sister! Come! Look!' he said, pulling them inside before Stella.

He pointed dramatically toward the showcase. 'See this! Our magic salt!'

Lucy's eyes widened.

'Uncle… it shines!' she squeaked, her little hands pressing against her cheeks.

Stella frowned at first, unsure what she was seeing, but curiosity soon softened her expression.

Lucy drew closer, transfixed.

'Can I take some, Uncle? Please?'

Dony ruffled her hair, unable to resist.

'Of course you can! Here… take half of it.'

He poured a portion of the glowing crystals into a piece of old newspaper and folded it carefully before handing it to her.

Lucy clutched it like a box of sweets.

Later, when Stella and Lucy returned to their block of apartments, even more neighbours gathered around the glowing packet, drawn to its unearthly light like moths to a flame. Some touched it. Some whispered prayers. Some simply stared in silence, unable to explain what they felt.

By then, nearly hundred people, men, women, children, had seen the "magic salt."

The days that followed were, at first, ordinary.

Jainagar Colony bustled with its usual rhythm, women returning from domestic work, men sorting scrap, children shrieking in the dusty courtyard. The glowing salt was a novelty, a topic of gossip and excitement, a strange distraction in a life otherwise shaped by monotony and hardship.

Lucy, six years old, small and curious, was the first to be taken by it.

It happened on a blistering afternoon. Stella had just finished washing clothes in a bucket when she saw her daughter sitting on the floor near the showcase, humming a tune, the packet of glowing salt open beside her.

'Lucy… what are you doing?' Stella's voice rose sharply.

Lucy looked up, smiling, her small face streaked with shimmering dust. Her cheeks were covered with the salt and her arms coated as if she had smeared glitter all over herself. She looked ethereal.

'Mommy! Look! Make-up!' she giggled, rubbing more of the powder on her forehead. 'Like the princesses in the stories!'

Lucy only laughed and ran off to play, swallowing pieces of rice with the same hand that had been dipped in the glow. A few grains of salt disappeared into her eager mouth without her even noticing.

Titus had been coughing since the night he saw Joy's

corpse, but he blamed the dust from the shop. He felt tired, but work demanded he show up. So he did.

Then the rashes started.

Blue-tinted rashes, like faint bruises shaped like tiny fingerprints. His wife noticed them first.

'You must go to the clinic,' she insisted.

'It's nothing,' Titus muttered.

But the rashes grew. Then they blistered and released thin, watery pus.

'Jesus… Jesus… Jesus… what is this…'

He went to the mirror and saw that his eyes, once yellowed from years of drinking, now had faint blue rings around the edges of his irises. He blinked hard.

The rings remained.

Dony's decline was worse.

He woke one morning screaming, his fingers burning with a strange cold fire. When his mother rushed to him, she saw the tips of his nails turning black. He found his upper thigh where he usually keeps his wallet, also burnt and decayed. The skin on his palm had begun to crack, as if something inside was sucking the moisture from it. When he tried to flex his fingers, the skin tore.

Within two days, Titus collapsed in his shop. He died before anyone could reach him.

Dony died that same night.

He screamed until his voice broke. His fingers decayed into blackened stumps and when he whispered his last breath.

The colony was drenched in shock.

People whispered. People stood in clusters, muttering about demons, curses, angels and punishments. Rumours spread faster than the sickness.

Two days later, more residents began falling ill. At first, they thought it was the food. Then the water. Then the heat.

Until their bodies began to betray them.

Children woke screaming in the night as their fingertips went numb. Men rubbed their eyes until they bled, complaining of strange lights dancing in their vision. Women found patches of skin turning pale, then cracking, then glowing faintly. Doors shut early. The streets emptied. Even the dogs stayed silent.

People whispered about the glowing salt as if it were a cursed mythical relic. Some said it came from a fallen star. Some insisted it was a demon seed. Whatever it was, the fear spread thicker than the sickness.

Stella watched it all spiral around her. But the terror in her own house was worse. Lucy was no longer the playful child she had been. She grew tired. So tired that she slept for hours, waking only to complain of headaches. Her skin grew unnaturally warm. Her eyes looked sunken. A faint blue tint lingered beneath her fingernails. Worst of all, she sometimes stared into empty corners of the room, whispering to someone who wasn't there.

'Lucy… who are you talking to?' Stella asked one night.

Lucy pointed to the darkest corner of the room, her voice barely audible.

'The shining lady.'

Stella froze.

Stella pulled her daughter into her arms and cried silently into her hair.

She knew children imagined things but this felt different. This felt wrong.

Pastor Isaac, tall, with an intense gaze, called an emergency meeting at the colony's prayer hall.

Hundreds gathered, coughing, scratching their rashes, shielding their eyes from phantom lights. The pastor stood on the stage, raising his hands dramatically.

'Brothers and sisters, listen! The Devil has entered our colony!'

A murmur ran through the crowd.

'The glowing object… the so-called "magic salt"… it is cursed! Cursed by the Devil himself! Anyone who touched it, anyone who kept it, has opened the gates to suffering!'

Women cried. Men trembled.

'Do NOT go to hospitals!' Pastor Isaac thundered. 'Doctors will not understand this! Medicine cannot cure what the Devil has marked! Only prayer can heal us!'

A wave of terrified nodding swept through the crowd.

'Bring your sick! Bring your children! I will perform healing sessions every night until the curse is lifted! God will save us!'

And no one dared question him.

But each night, as he prayed loudly, pressing trembling palms onto foreheads, chanting over writhing bodies, the sick grew worse.

Hands decayed. Visions intensified. Skin cracked and glowed. Children fainted.

The fear became a living creature, crawling through the colony, whispering nightmares into every ear. And Stella reached her breaking point.

One night, Lucy collapsed in the middle of prayer. Her body shook violently. Her small fingers curled unnaturally.

'PASTOR! HELP HER!' Stella screamed.

But Pastor Isaac stepped back, eyes wide, sweating.

'She… she is deeply cursed,' he stammered. 'I need time. I must pray. Do not go to a hospital until I receive divine instruction!'

Stella felt something break inside her.

She carried Lucy home, sobbing, trembling, shaking uncontrollably. Her mind spiralled, fear, confusion, guilt, desperation.

Stella sat beside her sleeping daughter all night, whispering prayers, tears streaming down her face. She felt trapped in a nightmare.

She felt dizzy, suffocated, trapped.

Then she saw something.

A video. A statement.

A man on TV proclaiming, boldly, clearly:

"There are no curses."

Dr. Markandeyan.

CHAPTER SEVEN
Sinners

The moment Stella finished her story, the consulting room seemed to shrink. Mark sat motionless, his hands clasped together. Stella, despite the tears in her eyes, straightened her back slightly.

'So… do you believe in curses now, Doctor?' she asked, her voice quivered with a strange mixture of triumph and despair.

Mark didn't answer immediately. The weight of her tale pressed deep into his chest. He had heard countless stories, seeing ghosts in their bedrooms, women convinced their neighbours cursed them, entire families possessed by ancestral demons. In every case, the cause was psychological, chemical, medical or environmental.

But this was an entire colony collapsing.

He exhaled slowly.

'Stella,' he said quietly, 'first of all… if any of you had gone to a proper hospital, a doctor would have diagnosed the exact cause. They would have run blood tests-'

She cut him off sharply.

'Hospital? There's no point,' she said, almost scoffing. 'Hospitals cheat. Medicines poison. Vaccines are scams. In our colony, disease is healed by prayer. Always has been. And Joy did go to a clinic. They said "food poison". What good was that?'

Her voice cracked and anger wrapped around grief like a thorny vine.

Mark inclined forward slowly.

'Stella… you must go to a doctor. Blood tests, scans, modern medicine can identify exactly what is happening. Whatever this is, there will be a scientific explanation.'

She shook her head.

'Pastor Isaac said the salt is cursed… the Devil is testing us…' she whispered, as though repeating words that frightened even her.

'Forget the pastor for now,' he said, firm. 'As for this "cursed salt", I need to see it myself.'

He had seen such cases before. Usually the "cursed object" turned out to be a rusted trinket, a plastic toy, a misinterpreted marking. Shared psychosis spread fear like fire in tightly knit groups. Human minds connected by belief could twist ordinary objects into supernatural threats.

This salt was probably nothing.

Maybe the colony's suffering came from contaminated water, sewage leakage, fungus, toxic dust…anything.

'I still have my share of it,' Stella wiped her eyes. 'At home. Pastor Isaac told us to keep it away, locked up. And the rest… the rest is in Titus's shop.'

'Good,' said Mark, rising from his chair. 'Then we go there. Now.'

'Now?' she asked. She glanced at the dark window. 'It's almost night…'

Mark picked up his car keys.

'Curses,' he said dryly, 'don't keep office hours.'

Stella stiffened.

'Let's go by my car,' he said.

'No, no… not in your car,' she said hurriedly, shaking her head, her face grew offended. 'I'll come on my own. By bus. We'll meet there at the East Gate of the colony.'

Mark didn't insist.

In this fragile social climate, a woman from Stella's colony being seen in another man's car, even for help, could be twisted into something disgraceful. Her pastor could excommunicate her. Her neighbours could shame her family.

Mark nodded respectfully.

'Very well,' he said.

Stella stood, clutching her bag close to her chest.

'I'll be there,' she whispered. 'Please… don't be late.'

Mark exhaled, rubbing his temples.

Ashok spoke softly. 'Sir… this sounds very serious.'

'Yes,' Mark murmured, staring at the doorway Stella had exited through. 'Too serious.'

They locked the house.

Outside, the city night blossomed. A warm breeze carried distant traffic sounds.

Mark and Ashok stopped at a tea shack before leaving. The owner lifted a hand in greeting, unaware that the two men were preparing to walk into a place no doctor had yet touched.

The car rolled through the road leading to Jainagar Colony. The largest slum in the state was cramped, dense, coiled like a serpent of concrete, tin, asbestos and desperation.

Mark and Ashok were sitting inside their car when they saw Stella walking towards the East Gate. They got out.

'Come…' she said and walked ahead.

Mark and Ashok walked behind her.

Jainagar Colony revealed itself long before Mark reached the gate. The transition from the city's orderly grid to the chaotic sprawl of the colony was abrupt.

Minutes earlier, Mark and Ashok had been cruising through well-lit roads lined with polished apartment complexes, cafés glowing with warm yellow light and neatly trimmed hedges guarding the pavements. The city centre was familiar, civilised, almost predictable, its air conditioned interiors, marble floors, glass facades and efficient traffic lights forming the silent background of Mark's everyday life. The buildings were clean, the drains were covered and the shops breathed a quiet assurance that everything was under control.

The streetlights here in Jainagar Colony flickered sporadically. The smooth asphalt gave way to cracked patches and uneven mud-streaked surfaces. Garbage bins overflowed at the roadside, spilling out plastic wrappers, vegetable waste and rusted utensils. Stray dogs darted between shadows with visible ribs.

The lanes were compressed, claustrophobic, squeezed by rows of two- and three-storey buildings whose paint had long peeled away. Some were cement-grey, others blotched with fungus, all scarred by years of monsoon rot. There were huge posters and cut-out figures of Malayalam and Tamil film stars. Clotheslines criss-crossed overhead like tangled nerves. Electrical wires hung dangerously low, some sparking faintly in the damp air.

Ridged asbestos sheets, stained bricks, rusted metal grills bent into makeshift gates. Water trickled from a broken pipe near a tea stall, forming a stagnant puddle where mosquitoes danced in grim delight.

Yes, the asbestos roofing sheets.

People feared curses, demons, invisible spirits, but the

true invisible killer was lodged right above their heads.

Mark knew exactly what those roofs meant. Every dry afternoon, when the wind scraped across those brittle panels, asbestos fibres, thin as dust, sharp as needles, would drift into the air. The colony breathed them in without ever knowing. The fibres lodged in lungs and stayed there for decades, quietly laying foundations for cancers and fatal scarring. A slow death, disguised as poverty's normalcy.

Children grew up playing under those roofs, women cooked beneath them, men slept inches away from them. Illness here wasn't an event, it was an environment. And the worst part, Mark thought bitterly, was that no one in places like this ever suspected asbestos. They blamed food, water, fate, ghosts, anything but the real culprit.

But today, he knew there is something else than asbestos to blame for.

Doors half-closed. Faces peered from behind rusted railings. These were people unused to outsiders. But this is no stranger. This was a man whose videos had travelled through their cracked phone screens, the man Pastor Isaac once warned them about during Sunday prayer.

Mark felt the weight of those eyes. Stella walked a little faster, head bowed, as though escorting a dangerous animal rather than a doctor.

Within ten minutes, shadows detached from the alleyways, five, maybe eight men, shoulders squared, blocking the path.

A thick-set man stepped forward, his eyes hard.

'Where do you think you're going?'

Mark paused. He looked at Stella, letting her speak.

'He… he wants to see the cursed salt,' she said quietly.

Murmurs rippled through the group.

'Are you mad?' the man spat. 'Don't you know who he is? This one… he speaks against God. We've seen his videos.'

Before Mark could answer, an engine growled from behind. A motorcycle screeched to a halt, dust rising around the rider like smoke. Pastor Isaac dismounted with the authority of a man accustomed to obedience.

'I came as soon as you called,' he said to the thick-set man, then turned sharply towards Mark.

His stare carried a rehearsed hatred.

'You have no business here,' the pastor said coldly. 'Leave.'

'Pastor,' one of the men protested, 'Stella brought him.'

'I… I only wanted to show him the cursed salt. To prove him wrong,' Stella faltered.

'There is no place here for a Satanist to wander,' the pastor replied.

'A what?' Mark blinked.

'A Satanist,' Isaac repeated firmly. 'Anyone who speaks against God is aligned with Satan. And you-' he jabbed a finger, 'you mislead the people with lies wrapped in science.'

'I don't believe in Satan,' Mark said, trying to keep his voice steady. 'does that make me a believer in God?'

A few men hissed. Others stepped closer. The air pulsed with rising anger.

'I'm here because your people are sick,' Mark continued. 'Your children are sick. You have a health crisis-'

'Then answer this, we will let you pass then' Pastor Isaac snapped. 'Do you believe God created the world?'

Mark held his gaze.

'No.'

Shouts burst from every direction.

'Blasphemer!'

'Devil's man!'

'Get out of our colony!'

Ashok flinched as the crowd surged a step forward, fists clenched, eyes burning with indoctrinated fury.

Pastor Isaac raised a hand like a judge delivering a sentence.

'Leave. Now.'

Mark glanced at Stella. She stood rigid, trembling, torn between fear for her daughter and fear of her own people. Their eyes met only for a moment, hers full of helpless apology.

Mark exhaled slowly.

'Alright. We're leaving.'

But before he stepped away, he leaned closer to Stella, voice low but urgent.

'If you love your daughter… go to the hospital. Do not wait.'

Stella's lips parted, but no sound emerged.

Mark turned. He and Ashok walked back through the narrow lane.

Mark paused at the gate and looked back. The narrow lanes of the colony had already folded into darkness. It felt as if the place itself had withdrawn, curling inward like a wounded animal.

A hopeless place.

For a brief moment, that thought stung him. But Mark wasn't one to surrender easily.

'Let's circle the perimeter,' he said quietly.

Ashok responded with a quiet acknowledgement and eased the car forward, navigating the uneven road that traced the slum's boundary. The sodium streetlights flickered intermittently which threw patches of light onto puddles and garbage heaps.

After a few minutes, Mark suddenly shifted forward.

'Stop… stop… stop.'

Ashok braked. Mark stepped out immediately.

Across the road loomed a huge, derelict structure. Tall, grey, hollow. Its windows were black rectangles, like empty eye sockets staring out at nothing. A forgotten hospital, lost beneath vines and mould. There was not a single light inside.

They crossed the road and walked up to a rusted gate. An old security guard sat slumped in a plastic chair, illuminated only by the bluish glow of his smartphone. Some comedy clip blared from his earbuds; he laughed loudly, shaking his head.

'Excuse me,' Mark called politely. 'What building is this?'

The guard barely looked up.

'Old hospital,' he said, already returning to his phone.

'What happened to it?'

'Court case… disputes… shut down. No one allowed inside.' He waved a dismissive hand, irritated Mark had interrupted his amusement.

'Can we enter and take a look?'

'No. Not even the owners allowed until court says so,' the guard grumbled, eyes glued to the screen.

'When was it-'

The guard suddenly snapped.

'Please! I said no! Go away! Don't disturb me.'

Mark sighed. He exchanged a glance with Ashok.

'Let's go.'

They walked back to the car, but they had barely moved fifty metres when Mark spoke again.

'Stop.'

Ashok halted.

'What happened?'

Mark stared at the silhouette of the abandoned hospital through the windshield.

'Ashok… we have to get inside.'

'Inside?' Ashok's voice rose an octave. 'Why?'

'Something about that building connects to the colony's sickness. Sewage leak, chemical dump, environmental hazard… something. Whatever it is, we can't wait for government procedures. Those people are dying by the week.'

Ashok's voice caught. 'But the guard, he won't let us—'

'Who said anything about the main gate?'

Mark tapped the dashboard.

'We climb the wall. He's too engrossed in his phone to notice a bomb going off, let alone us slipping in.'

'I suppose we're taking… equipment?' Ashok groaned.

'Obviously.'

Mark popped the trunk. He always carried a sealed emergency box. Heavy-duty torches, N95 masks, gloves, basic tools. Ashok held one mask loosely, eyeing the hospital like it might bite.

'We're entering an abandoned medical facility,' Mark said. 'Masks on. Old hospitals breed all sorts of pathogens.'

Ashok muttered, 'Lovely,' and put the mask on.

He parked near the boundary wall, where an overgrown mango tree cast deep shadows. Using the car roof as a makeshift platform, they climbed and dropped down into the compound.

It was pitch black.

The air was damp, thick with the smell of mould, rotting leaves and long-decayed disinfectant. Crickets chirped somewhere in the distance but the building itself stood dead silent. They walked for a few minutes before reaching the main entrance. Four large glass doors with iron grills were chained and sealed by official notices peeled by rain and time.

Ashok's sigh fogged his mask.

'Mark, let's go home. Really. You saw the gate. We can't get in.'

Mark raised an eyebrow.

'Are you scared?'

'Aaaah… yeah,' Ashok admitted helplessly. 'Old haunted-looking hospital? At night? With broken windows and blood-stained tiles? Of course I'm scared.'

Mark chuckled softly.

'I thought after all our investigations together, ghosts wouldn't bother you.'

'It's not ghosts,' Ashok hissed. 'It's the ambience. This place screams *run*. And you're telling me not to be scared?'

'You're with me,' Mark said, pushing aside a dead creeper hanging from a wall. 'If anything should scare you… it's snakes.'

Ashok stiffened.

'You're not helping.'

Mark walked ahead, scanning the facade with his flashlight. Suddenly he stopped.

A window gaped open, glass shattered outward, grills bent, as if someone had used force from inside.

'Someone's been using this place,' Mark murmured. 'Often.'

They moved closer. Vines curled through the broken window frame like skeletal fingers. Mark peered up, assessing the climb.

'We're going in,' he said.

Ashok faltered again but followed him loyally, as always.

With effort, the two of them climbed through the broken window, landing on a dusty corridor filled with toppled wheelchairs, peeling paint and hospital charts fluttering slightly in the night breeze.

Ashok's flashlight trembled in his hand.

'Mark… this looks exactly like those Hollywood horror movies.'

Mark smirked.

'Good. Then you already know what to expect.'

'That doesn't help either,' Ashok whispered, inching closer.

Ashok's footsteps crunched on broken tiles. Mark, moving ahead with his flashlight low, scanned everything with the precision.

They navigated an old corridor, its ceiling sagging like dead skin. The smell was an assault with mould, stale disinfectant and something metallic lingering beneath it. Their flashlight beams danced along walls littered with old posters of smiling nurses and outdated health slogans, peeling like dried scabs.

A sudden clatter echoed from somewhere in the darkness.

Ashok froze. 'What was that?'

Mark steadied the beam. 'Probably a fallen ceiling tile… rats… maybe a civet.'

'You always say "maybe". I hate your "maybe",' Ashok complained.

Mark only continued walking.

Another clatter - louder, sharper.

Ashok's voice cracked. 'Doc, that's not a rat. That walked.'

Mark didn't respond. They reached a corner smeared with water stains. Ahead, the corridor split into two - left downed in pitch darkness, right framed by a moonlight that somehow still had life in it.

Mark noticed something on the floor.

Tracks. Footwear marks… and small circles of disturbed dust.

Someone walked here recently.

He crouched, examining carefully. 'Ashok,' he said, 'this hospital… it's not just abandoned. Someone has been entering this place in the last few days or weeks.'

Ashok groaned into his palms. 'Of course. Why not? Ghosts are too basic. Let's add intruders also.'

They took the left passage, the deeper, darker one. The corridor narrowed. Paint hung in flakes like dead moth wings. Every few metres, a rusted wheelchair sat abandoned.

A sudden metallic squeal.

Both men jerked their flashlights upward.

A dangling IV pole, hanging by a thread of wire, slowly rotated.

Mark angled his light down the hallway, scanning shadows for movement. 'Calm down. Wind through broken windows can move objects.'

Before he replied, a shape flickered at the edge of the light. Ashok saw a pale blur, almost like a figure standing the far end of the corridor.

'There's someone standing over there. Look,' Ashok murmered.

Mark moved forward without hesitation, the beam steady, his posture rigid with focus. Ashok followed reluctantly.

When they reached the end of the corridor they found-

Nothing.

Just a half-collapsed wall and an overturned gurney.

A false scare.

'Pareidolia. Your brain is filling in shapes. Stress, darkness… it tricks vision easily,' Mark exhaled.

Ashok pinched the bridge of his nose. 'Yeah. Sure. Good. Let's go home.'

But Mark wasn't listening anymore.

They turned around and explored the other corridor. A faint dripping echoed, rhythmic, hollow, like water falling into a deep well. The further they walked, the colder the air grew. Their flashlights cut narrow tunnels through the darkness, illuminating corners filled with broken stretchers and shattered glass.

Then the corridor widened abruptly, opening into a vast hall.

The oncology waiting area.

'This isn't an ordinary hospital,'Mark whispered.

'What do you mean?' Ashok blinked.

'This was a radiotherapy centre. A cancer treatment facility.'

Shadowy chairs were lined in rigid rows like silent mourners waiting for a funeral no one would attend. Faded posters of cancer awareness hung crookedly on the walls. In the dim light, the smiling faces looked warped and sinister.

'I have a bad feeling about this. I need to confirm if my theory is right,' said Mark.

'You already formulated a theory?' asked Ashok.

'Ahead,' Mark said firmly. 'The radiotherapy unit must be through that wing.'

They headed towards a heavy metal door with the radiation warning symbol, a faded yellow trefoil with peeling black spokes.

The door was half-open.

That should have been impossible.

Radiation rooms were sealed shut with reinforced locks.

Even abandoned, they remained secure… unless someone had pried it open.

When Mark pushed the door, it groaned like a dying animal.

Inside, the floor was littered with broken lead tiles.

'Lead… why would someone tear out lead tiles?' Ashok froze.

'Because lead blocks radiation. Someone might have ripped it out to steal. Probably Joy and Mebin.' Mark felt cold spread in his chest.

He raised his flashlight.

The room was cavernous. Thick walls. A control booth behind glass. And, at the centre…

'The treatment chamber,' Mark whispered.

The bunker-like cylinder stood cracked open, its protective

shielding twisted like cheap metal. The steel door hung by a single hinge.

A pit in the floor was visible, a capsule-sized cavity, now empty and scorched around the edges, like something had been wrenched free with brute force.

'GET OUT!' shouted Mark in desperation.

'What! What happened?' asked Ashok.

'We shouldn't be here,' said Mark in desperation. 'We should leave NOW!'

As they raced back through the dark hallways, the hospital around Mark began to twist. The peeling walls blurred. The flickering lights dimmed. Footsteps echoed strangely. As they ran back, Mark heard someone calling in the hospital corridor.

A sharp ringing filled his ears.

Then-

A woman's voice.

Soft. Familiar. Heartbreaking.

'Mark…'

He stopped mid-run.

His flashlight flickered.

Ashok skidded to a halt a few steps ahead. 'Mark? MARK!'

But Mark wasn't hearing him anymore.

He was staring down the corridor - where a figure now stood.

A woman in a pale hospital gown.

Hair tied back exactly as she used to wear it.

Hands resting on her pregnant belly.

His wife.

Alive.

Smiling calmly at him.

A vision, impossibly vivid.

Mark's breath strangled in his throat.

Her form flickered - faint, like a reflection in broken glass.

Now he could hear the baby crying.

His flashlight slipped from his hand.

Ashok grabbed him, shaking him hard. 'DR MARK!'

He then he slapped Mark.

*

The Church of Jainagar Colony stood pressed between two blocks of concrete apartments like a rib wedged between lungs. The building was modest, corrugated iron roofing, walls painted a fading sky-blue, but tonight it pulsed with life. The air inside was thick, humid, vibrating with voices, bodies and fear.

People squeezed shoulder to shoulder, filling every plastic chair, every aisle, the space behind the pulpit. The LED bulbs illuminated the hall evenly.

At the centre of this storm stood Pastor Isaac, elevated on the stage.

The clean-shaven man was particularly excited today. He wore his trademark white shirt and a long silk tie.

Tonight, his expression was triumph and terror tied together.

He snatched the microphone from its stand.

A hush fell instantly.

Pastor Isaac lifted his free arm dramatically as though pulling invisible curtains.

'My children…' he began with a very scratchy voice. 'We gather here… not in joy… but in danger.'

A collective murmur passed through the crowd. Stella felt her stomach tighten. She had left her daughter Lucy alone at home. Lucy was in an unconscious state.

She had heard this tone from the pastor before, during storms, during deaths, during every crisis the colony had ever faced. His voice always slithered perfectly between warning and prophecy.

Pastor Isaac continued.

'We all know,' he said, raising his volume, 'what the cursed salt has brought upon us.'

People shook their heads, some weeping, some nodding vigorously.

A mother cried out, Pastor, my son's skin is burning!

Another shouted, My eyes! My eyes are hurting! My vision is fading!

Pastor Isaac pressed a hand to his chest, eyes closed.

'Yes… yes, my children… I know.'

He opened his eyes again.

'Only if Joy and Mebin were alive,' he declared, pacing slowly across the stage, 'we would have known from which wretched place they got it. Only if they were with us, we would have had the truth.'

He paused dramatically.

'BUT!' Isaac roared suddenly. 'They are GONE! Taken from this world! Swept away by the DEVIL HIMSELF!'

A ripple of gasps.

'HALLELUJAH!' someone shouted.

'Glory! Glory!' others chanted.

'Hallelujah!' the crowd roared louder.

The church shook with their voices.

Pastor Isaac raised both hands again, like a conductor summoning a storm.

'My children!' he thundered. 'Joy and Mebin were BETRAYED! Tricked! Fooled by Satan! The cursed salt was given to them by the Devil. Just as he deceived Eve with the forbidden fruit!'

The crowd moaned, rocking on their feet.

'We have fallen into the same sin!' he shouted. 'We touched it! Smelled it! KEPT it! SHOWED it!'

Hands covered mouths in shame.

'And what has happened?' he cried. 'Burning skin! Decay! Headaches! Blindness! Suffering!'

'YES, PASTOR!' voices answered in unison.

'It is our TEST!' Isaac roared. 'Our TRIAL!'

An old man collapsed to his knees, sobbing.

A woman beside Stella beat her chest, wailing, 'Forgive us, Oh Lord! Forgive us!'

Stella thought of the glowing salt. The strange burn marks on Dony's hands before he died. The way everyone was falling sick so quickly.

But the pastor's voice cut through her thoughts once more.

Pastor Isaac suddenly dropped the microphone.

People gasped.

His body trembled. His eyes rolled upwards. His lips moved as though speaking in tongues. He doubled over, shaking violently.

Then, he screamed.

A thin, shrill sound that sliced the air.

Women clutched their chests. Men bowed their heads. Some began shouting prayers in a frenzy.

'Pastor! Pastor! God is speaking to him!'

'The Lord is upon him!'

'Hallelujah! Hallelujah!'

Stella felt dread rise inside her like cold water. She had seen this performance countless times.

Every possession, every revelation, followed the same pattern. But tonight, it felt too dangerous. Too reckless. People were dying. Her daughter was burning up back home.

We need a doctor just like Dr Mark said, she thought desperately. Not a sermon. Not a ritual. A doctor. A real one.

But she dared not speak it aloud.

The pastor straightened suddenly with blazing eyes.

He snatched the microphone again, panting.

'YES!' he screamed. 'YES, HE HAS SPOKEN TO ME!'

He pointed upward dramatically.

'THE LORD HAS SPOKEN!' he announced.

'Hallelujah!'

'Praise the Lord!'

He walked in circles on the stage, trembling, yelling fragmented words.

'CURSE!'

'DEVIL!'

'PUNISHMENT!'

'REPENT!'

Then he stopped at the centre, raised his hand, and declared-

'God has shown me the way!'

A gasp went through the hall like a tidal wave.

'He has given me the SOLUTION!'

More gasps.

'He has instructed ME!'

People began crying openly.

'Save us, pastor! Save us!'

Pastor Isaac's voice thundered over them.

'Tomorrow,' he announced, 'when the sun hits noon… I shall take the cursed salt in my hands…' he paused for dramatic effect, '…and I shall DROP IT into the river!'

The crowd exploded.

'HALLELUJAH!'

'THE CURSE WILL END!'

'THE LORD WILL SAVE US!'

'GLORY! GLORY!'

People jumped, danced, prayed screamed.

Pastor Isaac waved his arms, feeding the frenzy.

'The Devil has no place among us! God will drown his

power! The river shall carry our sins away!'

But Stella sat frozen. A cold, heavy dread spread through her bones.

This is wrong. This isn't divine. It's dangerous. This salt… whatever it is… it's killing us. And drowning it in the river?

Her mind raced through images of people bathing in that river. Children playing. Water flowing to other neighbourhoods.

It could spread. It could contaminate more.

She remembered Dr Mark's calm voice.

Pastor Isaac raised his palms once more, commanding silence.

'Children of God,' he said dramatically, 'return home. Pray. Prepare. Tomorrow, the curse shall be broken. Tomorrow, you shall break open Titus's scrap shop and give me the Cursed Salt so that I can dispose it just like our Lord instructed.'

The crowd began dispersing, still chanting, still trembling with emotion.

But Stella remained seated. Frozen.

CHAPTER EIGHT
Rays of Despair

Mark woke with a violent jolt, as though some invisible hand had yanked him upward from a nightmare. His pulse hammered. His throat felt parched. For a moment, he couldn't even remember where he was.

Not the hospital. Not the ruined corridors. Not the visions.

Then the door creaked open.

Ashok stepped in quietly, holding a steaming cup of tea in both hands. His shirt was rumpled, hair messy, as though he hadn't slept at all.

'Oh… you woke,' he said softly.

'What… what happened last night?' Mark rubbed his face with trembling fingers.

Ashok placed the cup on the table beside him.

'We were at that radiotherapy centre …' Ashok hesitated. '…you had those visions again.'

Mark shuddered.

'It took me a great deal of trouble to drag you out,' Ashok

continued, voice weary. 'You fainted twice. And convincing the security…I had to pay the old man five thousand bucks to let us move without a scene. Somehow managed to get you into the car and bring you here.'

Mark sat up abruptly.

'Radiotherapy centre!' he said, the memory crashing back violently. He swung his legs off the bed. 'Oh shit. Ashok, listen to me carefully.'

'What now?' Ashok frowned.

'Take everything we wore last night, everything. Clothes, shoes, the gloves, even the underwear.' Mark's voice had risen to an urgent, almost panicked pitch. 'Collect it all and dump it. No, bury it. Deep. And we need lead sheets. We must wrap everything in lead before burying.'

'What? Why? Are we… are we infected?' Ashok stared, horrified.

Mark looked at him, eyes glassy, haunted.

'My doubts were right,' he whispered. 'I know what the cursed salt is.'

'What?'

Mark stood, pacing in frantic circles. 'Even we are affected from being inside that radiation room.'

'Hold on, hold on.' Ashok raised both hands. 'What? You believe in cursed items now?'

'No!' Mark barked. 'It's not cursed.' Then, more softly but trembling with desperation, 'It's something worse, Ashok. Much worse.'

He ran a hand through his hair, trying to breathe steadily.

'That powder,' he said, 'that glowing salt they were playing with, it's not magical. It's not demonic. It's radiation source material used for radiotherapy.' His throat tightened. 'Probably Cesium-137.'

Ashok froze, colour draining from his face.

'Cesium… you mean… radiation…? Real radiation?'

'Yes.' Mark settled back heavily against the wall. 'And from the look of that facility, the casing is broken. The source capsule is probably missing. Joy and Mebin must have taken it long ago. And it's out there, in the middle of a slum where children play with it like glitter.'

Ashok's lips parted but no words came.

'We went inside a contamination zone without protective gear,' Mark continued, his voice cracking. 'Jainagar Colony needs to be evacuated and the radioactive substance must be taken away.'

'But the colony, they won't let us in, remember?' Ashok shook his head helplessly.

'But this is no longer in our hands,' replied Mark.

He grabbed his phone with trembling fingers.

'This is the State's job now. This is an emergency.'

He began typing, breath shaky.

'We can't waste a second, Ashok. People will die. Children… women… the whole colony. Radiation poisoning is irreversible once it begins. And if that salt spreads through water or soil…I'm calling the Commissioner,' Mark said, in desperate voice. 'Right now.'

Mark's thumb hovered over the dial button. Commissioner Vikram's number glowed on the screen.. But just before he pressed, the phone buzzed violently in his hand.

An incoming call.

Dr Akhil Kumar Taluk Hospital.

'Why is he calling this early?' he muttered under his breath.

'It's almost half past ten, doc. Just pick it up,' Ashok drew closer.

'No. He can wait. I have to call the Commissioner. That's urgent,' said Mark.

'Just take it,' insisted Ashok. 'Maybe it'll take a minute.'

Mark hesitated, then jabbed the green button.

'Hello?'

'Hello, doctor, I hope you're free?' Dr Akhil's voice came hurried, slightly breathless.

'I'm in the middle of a very urgent case. Can it wait?' replied Mark sharply.

'Just… just a minute. A patient…a lady…came in to consult me. She said you referred her but she doesn't have a note or prescription. She looks very troubled. I thought maybe you know her medical history. Feels like an emergency, that's why I called…'

Mark felt a cold spike race down his spine.

His throat tightened. 'Where is she?'

'She was taken to lie down in the Emergency. And…' Akhil hesitated. 'She brought something in a bag. Said it's responsible for her problems. Her daughter is also suffering but too unwell to come.'

Mark's surroundings faded. The walls, the light, the bed, all dissolved. He felt the gravitational pull of panic drag him inward like he was falling into a black hole.

'Where did you keep that bag?' Mark asked, voice stripped to a whisper.

'It's in the corner of my room,' said Dr Akhil, chuckling nervously. 'I didn't open it. I'm afraid it might be some snake or something.'

Ashok, listening on speaker, stared at Mark's ashen face.

Mark's vision swam. His knees weakened. For a moment, he thought the world tilted sideways.

'Dr Mark? You still there?' came Akhil's puzzled voice.

Mark pushed down the rising terror and kept his voice steady, deliberate.

'Listen to me very carefully, Dr Akhil.'

A long pause on the other end.

'What I am about to tell you is extremely serious. You must listen without interruption.'

Akhil exhaled, confused. 'O-okay…'

'The bag she brought contains a dangerous radioactive substance. Cesium-137 in crystal form. No lead casing. Nothing. The mere presence of it inside your hospital is enough to contaminate the entire building. Every person inside is at risk right now, including you.'

He heard the faint rustle of clothing and an abrupt gasp.

'R-radioactive…?' Akhil's voice dropped to a whisper.

'You must stop all consultations immediately,' said Mark, each word sharp as glass. 'Leave the room at once. Evacuate everyone near you. Call the Fire and Rescue Department for crowd control. Do not, under any circumstances, open the bag or touch it.'

Akhil stammered, 'But-'

'No time to listen to your reply,' Mark cut in. 'I will call the Energy Research Centre. And the City Commissioner. I'm leaving right now. Do exactly as I said, and do it fast. I'll be there.'

He ended the call with a trembling thumb.

For a moment, Mark just stood there, motionless, pale, drenched in dread.

Ashok stepped forward quietly.

'We are running out of time,' Mark said.

Mark's fingers trembled as he called Commissioner Vikram's number. The moment the call connected, he didn't waste even a breath.

He told Vikram everything. Every horrifying detail.

On the other end of the line, there was a long, stunned silence. Then the commissioner exhaled shakily.

'Tell me, Dr Mark… what should I do?' Vikram's voice, usually stern and immovable, now carried a tremor. 'I will arrange the entire state's machinery to solve this problem.'

'The people of Jainagar Colony are difficult to manage,' he said. 'They won't listen to outsiders. You must go with an entire force. Send an army of cops, Fire and Rescue teams… no delays. I'll tell someone from the Energy Research Centre to meet you there with a scintillation counter to detect radiation.'

He paused to steady his breath.

'They'll also bring as many hazmat suits as possible. Police must be protected from contamination. Meanwhile, I'm going to Taluk Hospital. I have to find Stella. I must learn where the rest of the Cesium-137 is.'

There was another short silence, but this time Vikram answered with the decisiveness of a commander receiving wartime orders.

'Will do that,' he said as though he were answering a superior officer. 'I will also open Jayachandran Nair Stadium for emergency rehabilitation. We'll shift the entire Jainagar Colony there. One by one, we'll run tests for radioactive contamination.'

Mark felt a sharp jolt of relief, like a breath after drowning.

'That's… that's great,' he said, exhausted.

The moment the call ended, the room buzzed with urgency.

Within half an hour Mark and Ashok burst out of the house, locked the door with a metallic clack and hurried to the car.

On the road, with sirens from distant police vans beginning to echo somewhere far behind them, Mark dialled the Energy Research Centre.

His voice was clipped, urgent, technical.

'We have a suspected Cesium-137 leak. Multiple exposures. Possible contamination of an entire settlement. I need one of your physicists at Taluk Hospital immediately- scintillation counters, Geiger-Müller tubes, protective suits… everything you can spare. This is priority one.'

On the other end, the physicist inhaled sharply.

'Understood, doctor. I'll be there soon.'

Ashok gripped the steering wheel tightly as they sped down the narrow district road. Mark sat in the passenger seat, breathing hard, fingers trembling slightly as he checked his phone again.

Ashok glanced at him.

'You look like you've seen a ghost, doctor,' he said quietly.

'I wish it were a ghost,' Mark shook his head.

'Then tell me what this is. What's Cesium-137? You said it's radiation… but how dangerous is it?' Ashok's voice came strained.

'Alright. Listen carefully. I need you to understand the gravity of this, Ashok, because we're walking straight into hell,' Mark exhaled sharply.

The car hit a pothole. Neither of them reacted.

'Cesium-137,' Mark continued, 'is a radioactive isotope created in nuclear reactors. It doesn't exist in nature. It's man-made. Highly energetic. Highly dangerous. It emits gamma radiation, penetrating radiation. The kind that burns through flesh, damages DNA and destroys internal organs silently.'

'But why is it in hospitals?' Ashok tightened his grip on the wheel.

'Because,' Mark said grimly, 'something this deadly can also be used to heal. In radiotherapy units, gamma beam therapy machines, Cs-137 is sealed inside a thick, shielded capsule. Patients with cancer are exposed to controlled beams of this radiation to shrink tumours.'

Ashok blinked rapidly. 'So… it's like using poison to kill poison.'

'Exactly. Controlled poison. Very controlled. Extremely

shielded.' Mark leaned closer. 'If that shielding breaks or if the source is removed from its container, it becomes a silent weapon. It irradiates everything around it. Clothing. Air. Soil. Food. Human bodies. Anything.'

'And what happens to people who get exposed?'

'That depends on dose and duration. What Stella described, skin peeling, ulcers, nausea, headaches, diarrhoea, burns, those are classic symptoms of radiation syndrome. High-dose external exposure or contamination.'

Mark paused and added, voice dropping lower, 'And that glowing salt they saw… that is the powdered ceramic that encases the Cs-137 source. It glows faintly because the radiation ionises the air around it. People think that glow is "magic" or "curse". It's actually pure death.'

'So anyone who touched it…?' Ashok asked waiting for bad news.

'Is in grave danger,' Mark said. 'They absorbed radioactive particles through their skin. Through cuts. Through their lungs. Through their food. Stella's daughter, Lucy, she put it on her skin and ate some. That is catastrophic exposure.'

Ashok's breath hitched. 'Oh God…'

'Keep driving,' Mark said calmly but urgently. 'We can't panic. We have to reach the hospital before more people touch that bag.'

Ashok nodded, forcing himself to focus on the road.

Mark continued, voice steadier now, slipping into the precise tone of a trained scientist trying to save lives.

'There are two types of danger with a source like this: external irradiation and internal contamination. External radiation is like being near an invisible furnace. You get burned from the outside. Internal contamination is far worse. It means the radioactive material has entered the body and will irradiate you from within, for as long as it remains inside.'

Ashok felt cold. 'And Lucy…?'

Mark closed his eyes for a moment. 'If she ingested even a milligram….she has undergone a slow painful death by now.'

The engine hummed. Rubber hissed on asphalt.

Ashok whispered, 'Doctor… how could this happen?'

Mark replied, 'Because that abandoned radiotherapy clinic wasn't dismantled properly. The Cs-137 source was still inside the broken machine. Joy and Mebin broke it out and sold it as scrap without knowing its danger.'

He turned to Ashok, face hollow.

'This is a level-7 radiological disaster waiting to happen.'

Ashok's breathing quickened. 'And we stepped inside the radiation room last night… without protection…'

Mark looked out the window, jaw clenched.

'Yes,' he said softly. 'We did.'

The car sped on.

'Gamma radiation doesn't just burn. It breaks molecules apart. Shatters DNA. Unravels cells. At high doses, it liquefies internal organs,' Mark said.

Ashok drew a sharp breath. 'So when we entered…'

'We got a low dose, enough to worry, not enough to kill. Stella's colony, however… they're facing cumulative exposure. Touching it. Carrying it. Living with contaminated clothes, contaminated soil, contaminated water. Some may have inhaled particles. That's fatal.'

Ashok tried to breathe, tried to steady himself.

'But why… why does this salt glow?' he asked.

Mark sighed. 'Because the Cs-137 source is usually sealed inside a ceramic pellet called cesium chloride, which looks exactly like salt. When the capsule breaks, the pellet crumbles into powder. It's incredibly soluble, incredibly dispersive. A nightmare. A "magic glow" to the untrained eye.' He paused. 'But the glow is Cherenkov light, blue light produced when high-energy particles pass through air or moisture.'

Ashok felt sick.

'So when Lucy put it on her skin-'

'It was like applying acid made of pure radiation,' Mark cut in. 'The decay particles would have penetrated her epidermis, damaging every layer of tissue.'

Ashok ran a hand over his face. 'Oh, Shit!'

'And when she ate it,' Mark added softly, 'that was catastrophic internal contamination. That is far worse.'

'What happens then?' Ashok whispered. 'What happens to others who are contaminated?'

'The radioactive particles lodge in soft tissues liver, spleen, bone marrow. They keep irradiating the organs from the inside, destroying blood cells, crippling the immune system. It leads to bleeding, infection, organ failure. Skin sloughs off. Hair falls out. Vision deteriorates. Neurological issues start. Eventually… the body collapses.'

Ashok's foot slipped slightly on the pedal.

'So the entire colony… all those people…'

'They will fall sick one by one,' Mark said. 'Some already have. Skin lesions, vomiting, neurological instability. What Stella described, hands decaying, is not superstition. It's beta burns. Radiation necrosis.'

'What happens if the cesium spreads further?' he asked.

Mark answered immediately:

'It will contaminate the soil. It will wash into the drainage. It will enter groundwater. It can spread on shoes, clothes, bus seats, school corridors. It can disperse like dust in wind. If not contained immediately, it could affect thousands.'

Ashok felt sweat trickling down his back.

'So this isn't just a colony disaster… it could become a city disaster.'

'Exactly,' Mark said.

They turned onto the final stretch toward the hospital. Sirens wailed faintly in the distance. Fire trucks or ambulances responding to some other morning emergency. But Ashok suddenly felt as if all emergency sirens in the world were not enough.

Mark and Ashok pulled into the parking lot of the Taluk Hospital. They saw a white van parked nearby. Across its side, painted in bold navy-blue, were the words 'ENERGY RESEARCH CENTRE – HAZARD RESPONSE UNIT', and on its windshield a glaring red placard: URGENT.

Mark stepped out with his breath catching from dread. A lone man was walking back from the hospital entrance, a handheld device clutched against his chest. His face was pale. The device's small screen flickered with an angry red glow.

Mark approached him swiftly.

'You must be from the ERC,' said Mark.

The man introduced himself. 'Satish, Radiation Safety Officer.' He lifted the device slightly with frustration. 'I think this counter is faulty. I switched it on right at the hospital gate and it jumped straight to "saturated." Must be a malfunction. I'll take another one.'

He shook the instrument hard, as though that might convince it to behave. Mark felt Ashok stiffen beside him. Satish hurried back to the van, pulled out a second scintillation counter from the cargo box and powered it on. The LCD blinked alive. The beeping tone was calm.

'This one's fine,' said Satish, more to himself than anyone else. He inhaled once, squared his shoulders and began walking toward the hospital gate.

Mark and Ashok followed, the three of them moving like men approaching a sleeping tiger.

The moment Satish stepped past the threshold of the outer gate, the device let out a shrill, rapid cascade of alarms.

The screen flashed red.

SATURATED.

Satish froze.

Mark felt his stomach drop like a stone.

Ashok instinctively stepped back.

Satish stared at them both, his face turning a ghostly grey.

'This… this means…' he stammered.

Mark finished the sentence for him. 'It means the reading is maxed out from the gate itself. The radiation here is already at the highest measurable level.'

Satish spoke with difficulty. 'Which… which implies contamination all the way out here.'

'Cesium-137 disperses like dust,' whispered Mark. 'Carried by air, clothes, touch, everything.'

Satish looked at him helplessly. 'Dr Mark… this is… this is national-emergency-level.'

Satish lowered the device slowly, as if afraid even the movement might trigger something worse. When he spoke again, his voice had the clipped precision of protocol.

'The hospital building must be evacuated now. Not in ten minutes. Not in five. Now.'

Mark pulled out his phone, his hands trembling. He dialled Commissioner Vikram.

'Commissioner,' he said, his voice deliberately steady, 'we have confirmation. The Taluk Hospital is contaminated at gate-level saturation. This has escalated beyond civil administration. Evacuation is mandatory.'

There was no pause on the other end, only the sound of Vikram erupting into action. Sirens began wailing in the distance, as if responding to his words.

At the same moment, Satish turned to the firefighters stationed near the ambulance bay.

'No one approaches the bag the woman brought!'

he shouted. 'I repeat, no one touches it. Keep everyone a minimum of thirty metres away. Seal the corridor. No exceptions.'

The firefighters glanced at one another, startled but obedient. They moved back, radios crackling to life, boots thundering across the pavement.

Mark felt a cold sweat slide down his spine. This was spiralling faster than he had imagined.

'Ashok,' he said quietly, 'we need to see Stella.'

'We can't go in,' replied Ashok.

'Do you have a spare hazmat suit?' Mark asked Satish. 'I need one.'

Satish handed over a hazmat suit.

'You stay here,' Mark said, turning to Ashok. 'We can't wait till she is evacuated. I'll go and ask her.'

Ashok said nothing, though his hands shook.

The hospital grounds descended into chaos, nurses rushing out, patients being wheeled into the sunlight, mothers clutching infants, alarms blaring and Satish shouting orders over the rising confusion. The entire Taluk Hospital had become a ticking bomb of invisible poison.

Meanwhile, in Jainagar Colony, the operation unfolded like a war effort.

Three full convoys had arrived, two from the Energy Research Centre, one packed with radiation specialists in hazmat suits and the others filled with police battalions and Kerala Fire & Rescue units. The air vibrated with the thrum of diesel engines, the metallic clatter of equipment and the rising murmur of a thousand uneasy residents staring from doorways and balconies.

Commissioner Vikram himself stepped out of the lead vehicle. He signalled the officers forward.

Loudspeakers crackled to life.

'Attention! Attention! This is a public safety order. The colony must be evacuated immediately. Move towards the East Gate in an orderly manner. This is for your safety. Do not panic. Follow the instructions of the police and fire personnel.'

The words boomed through the narrow lanes, echoing off asbestos roofs and concrete walls. But instead of obedience, a wave of agitation spread through the crowd.

People pushed forward, shouting.

'Why should we leave?'

'Pastor said it's a curse, not a disease!'

'This is our home! Who are you to tell us?'

'We won't allow outsiders to touch our things!'

The crowd roared, emboldened.

Firefighters formed a semi-circle, shields raised, urging them back. Hazmat-suited ERC officers moved in carefully, scanning the perimeter with scintillation counters that screamed continuously. The readings were off the charts.

Commissioner Vikram grabbed a megaphone, voice thundering over the chaos.

'Your lives are in danger. This is not superstition. This is radiation contamination. If you stay here, you will die. Your children will die. We are here to save you. Move! NOW!'

Silence struck the crowd like a slap.

Mothers clutched children. Elderly men stared at trembling hands. The reality of death, scientific, invisible, merciless, began to pierce the veil of belief. Or was it because the inhabitants were weak enough not to defend themselves.

Slowly, reluctantly, the evacuation began.

Inside the hospital, the corridors buzzed with panic. Nurses hurried past in masks while firefighters shouted instructions. Mark moved through it all in a bulky hazmat suit. He reached a junction and stopped a trembling junior nurse.

'Emergency ward?' Mark asked.

She pointed with gloved hands. 'Second door on the left, sir. But… be careful.'

Mark ran.

The Emergency was chaos, patients on stretchers being wheeled out, doctors arguing in low, frightened voices, monitors beeping erratically. Mark scanned each bed until he saw Stella lying pale and limp under a thin sheet. Her hair was dishevelled, her eyes half-open, unfocused, as though she were slipping in and out of consciousness.

He rushed to her side.

'It's me, Mark,' he said, lowering his face closer so she could see him through the foggy visor.

Stella blinked slowly, struggling to recognise him. Her lips trembled. 'The doctor here… he told me what the cursed salt was,' she whispered. 'I didn't know… it was a radiation thing. What will happen to my daughter? She's alone at home.'

'Our team has gone to Jainagar Colony. Everyone will be taken out and treated. I wanted to ask you something. The rest of the substance…is it in that scrap shop? Where is that shop?'

Stella struggled to speak. Tears welled in her eyes. 'Doctor… the rest of that thing … it isn't in the scrap shop anymore.'

Mark's pulse spiked. 'What? Then where is it?'

'Pastor Isaac… he said he would dispose of it in the river,' she whispered.

For a moment, Mark felt like the world dropped out from under him.

'Stella,' he said sharply, leaning closer, 'I need his number. Right now. Please.'

She She gave a weak assent and fumbled with the sheet. 'Take… take my phone. It's in the pocket.'

Mark reached into the folded fabric and drew out a cheap keypad phone with a cracked screen. He glanced at Stella one last time. 'You're going to be alright. I'll handle this.'

He turned and hurried out of the ward.

Ashok was waiting near the entrance, half-suited, face tense with worry. Mark ripped off the hazmat hood, his hair drenched with sweat beneath it.

'What happened?' Ashok asked.

Mark's expression said everything before the words left his mouth. 'Pastor Isaac has the Cesium-137. He's planning to throw it into the river.'

Satish's face twisted in horror. 'Oh God! He's gonna dump it into the river? We must stop him!'

'I know.' Mark's fingers flew across the phone, trembling. 'I'm calling Commissioner Vikram. He needs the pastor's number now. They have to track him before he reaches the river.'

He hit the dial button, breathing hard, the weight of an entire city's fate pressing on him as the phone rang.

The road blurred beneath them as Ashok pushed the accelerator to its limit. Mark sat rigid in the passenger seat. In front of them, the van from the Energy Research Centre tailgated aggressively, its siren wailing.

'Any update from Vikram?' Ashok asked, eyes fixed on the road.

Mark checked the phone. 'They've traced Pastor Isaac's signal. He's heading towards the Chakkara Bridge.'

Ashok swore under his breath. 'The river…'

'If he drops the Cesium-137 into the Chakkara River,' Mark began, 'this city won't be the same again. Not for decades.'

'Decades?' Ashok whispered.

'If we're lucky,' Mark said. 'Ashok, water doesn't hide

radiation. It spreads it. Dilutes it, yes, but it spreads it endlessly. Every fish, every plant, every grain of silt at the bottom of the river will become contaminated. And when they decay or when people catch fish and eat them or when they irrigate their rice fields… the radiation enters their bodies.'

Ashok tightened his grip on the steering wheel. 'How bad are we talking?'

'This isn't fever or diarrhoea,' Mark replied. 'Cesium mimics potassium. The body absorbs it eagerly into blood, into muscles, into the heart. Once it's inside… it stays. It eats you slowly, cell by cell, molecule by molecule.'

Ashok felt something cold.

'Children will be the first to suffer,' Mark continued. 'Hair falling out. Skin sloughing off. Bone marrow shutting down. Tumours forming like wild growth. And pregnant women…' He looked away. 'Their babies will take the full load of that poison.'

Ashok swore under his breath. 'And the river flows into the backwaters… then to the sea…'

'Yes,' Mark said. 'And tens of thousands get their drinking water downstream. Imagine a slow invisible plague that no doctor can treat. Decades of cancer. Leukaemia. Birth defects. Whole families wiped out. Entire city dying without ever seeing the thing that killed them.'

The sky outside darkened as clouds gathered, heavy and swollen, the air thick with humidity.

'And even if we find the source later,' Mark added bitterly, 'we can't clean a moving river. Not fully. We'll spend years scraping sediment, closing water supply lines, evacuating communities, begging people not to touch the water their grandparents bathed in. It'll be a ghost river.'

Ashok's voice trembled. 'So if he drops it… it's apocalypse.'

'Yes,' said Mark. 'A slow apocalypse. The kind that doesn't

make noise. It doesn't explode. It whispers. It lingers. It ruins everything quietly.'

Ashok accelerated. 'Then we stop him. No matter what.'

Mark did not hesitate. 'We must. Because if that bag touches the water… it won't just be Jainagar Colony anymore. It'll be all of us.'

The phone buzzed. Commissioner Vikram.

'We have a lock on him,' Vikram said, breathless. Behind him, Mark could hear police sirens and radio chatter. 'He parked his motorcycle near the north end of the bridge. He is walking toward the centre. Looks like he's carrying a bag. We're two minutes away.'

'We're right behind you,' Mark replied.

They tore through the last bend leading to the river. The Chakkara Bridge stretched ahead. Old concrete pillars, sun-beaten, glistening under the unforgiving noon heat. At the far end, a lone figure walked slowly toward the centre, a jute grocery bag dangling from his hand.

'There!' Ashok pointed.

Pastor Isaac.

His long white shirt fluttered in the wind, and the grocery bag swung against his leg. The bag was ordinary. But everyone knew what was inside.

Death.

Ashok braked hard near the foot of the bridge. The ERC van screeched to a halt behind them. Fire and Rescue trucks rushed in from the opposite side. Police jeeps blocked both entrances.

Within seconds, the bridge was sealed.

Commissioner Vikram leapt from his vehicle. Officers spread out, palms outstretched, motioning bystanders away. The crowd began forming by the roadside. Mark ran forward with Ashok close behind. The ERC team pulled out radiation meters and began sweeping the air. The devices beeped angrily, red lights flashing.

'The radiation level is increasing!' an ERC physicist shouted. 'He's carrying it for sure!'

Pastor Isaac stopped walking. He turned slowly, staring at the line of officers approaching him. There was no fear in his eyes

'Pastor Isaac!' Vikram shouted through a loudspeaker. 'Put the bag down! Do not move!'

The pastor raised the bag slightly.

'Do not come near!' he shouted back. 'This cursed thing must be returned to the river. The Lord commanded me!'

Mark stepped forward instinctively, but Vikram caught his arm.

'Let me talk,' Mark said quietly.

'You can't go near him,' Vikram muttered. 'He has no idea what he's carrying-'

'Exactly why he'll listen to reason.' Mark pulled free and walked ahead.

Every step felt like walking through thick water. The bridge hummed with tension. The low rumble of engines, the beep of radiation counters, the murmurs of terrified officers seemed like an orchestra.

Mark stopped ten metres from the pastor. 'Pastor Isaac,' he called, raising his voice. 'Listen to me. That bag doesn't contain a curse. It contains Cesium-137.'

The pastor frowned. 'I don't care for your satanic science.'

'You will care,' Mark replied sharply. 'If that bag tears, if it falls, if it cracks even a little… you will burn. Not your soul, your body. Your flesh. And everyone around you.'

'I am obeying the Lord,' Pastor Isaac insisted.

'No,' said Mark firmly. 'You are obeying fear. And fear is not God. That substance is killing your people. It killed Joy.

It killed Mebin. It is hurting Stella. And it will kill Lucy.' Mark stepped forward. 'Do you want their deaths on your hands?'

The pastor's face twitched. His grip on the bag loosened slightly.

Vikram signalled the officers to hold position.

'Pastor,' Mark continued, stepping one more cautious pace closer, 'if you drop that into the river, even the Lord cannot save the thousands who drink that water. Children. Pregnant women. Your own congregation.'

The pastor looked down at the bag.

'Please,' Mark said quietly. 'Give me the bag. Let me help you.'

A long silence stretched across the bridge. The wind roared beneath them, carrying the smell of the river.

'Pastor Isaac!' Commissioner Vikram shouted, striding forward with a megaphone. 'Do not move! Put the bag down!'

But the pastor's eyes were wild, shining with delirious conviction. His face contorted, spittle flying as he raised the bag toward the river.

'I don't believe in you devils!' he screamed. 'I believe only in God! The Almighty commanded me to cast this SIN into the waters!'

The crowd of officers tensed. The ERC team froze mid-step. Even the wind seemed to hold its breath.

Pastor Isaac swung his arm back, muscles straining-

And in that split second, a gunshot cracked like thunder.

The pastor staggered as the bullet tore into his shoulder. His body twisted, crumpling toward the asphalt. But the bag, the *cursed bag*, remained in motion, slipping free, arcing through the air toward the railings.

'NO!' Mark shouted.

He ran.

Feet barely touching the road, he leapt. The world slowed,

the sirens, the screams, the sun itself, as Mark threw his entire body toward the tumbling grocery bag. His fingers caught it. The weight yanked him forward. His torso slammed against the railings. The metal bit into his ribs as gravity pulled him down, down toward the churning river.

'Mark!' Ashok roared.

Ashok lunged and caught Mark's shirt from behind. The fabric stretched, thread snapping like tiny screams. Two police officers rushed in, grabbing Mark's arms, hauling both men backwards. The bag slipped from Mark's sweaty grip for a heartbeat but he clutched it again, wrapping both hands around it in a desperate embrace.

Together they fell backwards onto the asphalt, gasping, shaking.

The ERC officers sprinted over at once.

'Careful! CAREFUL!' one of them yelled.

They unsnapped a lead-lined case with trembling hands. Mark thrust the bag forward. The physicists enclosed it swiftly, sealing it inside the thick lead coffin with a heavy clunk. Only then did Mark let his shaking fingers loosen.

Behind them, Pastor Isaac lay bleeding on the road, cradling his shoulder, his face twisted with pain and fury.

'You will answer for this on the Judgement Day!' he howled. 'You interfered with God's command! You devils!'

Commissioner Vikram walked over, eyes cold, voice firm as granite.

'And you' he said, 'will answer to a human judge in a court of law.'

The pastor's cries dissolved into the wail of sirens, the rush of river wind and the trembling breath of a city narrowly saved from catastrophe. Mark sat on the asphalt, chest heaving, sweat dripping from his hair. Ashok knelt beside him, still gripping his shoulder, as if afraid Mark might hurl himself into the river again.

The months that followed were some of the darkest the state had faced in decades. A thick unease settled over the district like a slow-moving storm, heavy and oppressive. Every newspaper headline carried the same stark imagery: evacuation tents, hazmat suits, Geiger counters and a colony erased by an invisible poison. The Taluk Hospital at the centre of the catastrophe stood abandoned as its gates chained, its windows sealed with warning notices and radioactive hazard symbols.

The government shut it down indefinitely.

At the stadium-turned-relief centre, the displaced families of Jainagar Colony lived in rows of white tents flapping in the monsoon wind. Doctors in protective suits moved from person to person, testing each for contamination.

Families waited in long lines, clutching documents, holding trembling children and bags of belongings they had hurriedly gathered before evacuation.

As the night deepened, more tents filled with bodies. Some died screaming. Some crying. Some praying. Many in numb confusion.

By dawn, twenty-two from Jainagar Colony were dead. By evening, the number reached forty-seven. Over the next days, it crossed a hundred. The news channels camped outside the stadium gates. The entire state was watching. Every headline screamed variations of the same horror:

MYSTERY SUBSTANCE KILLS ENTIRE COLONY

PASTOR'S ACTION CAUSES RADIOACTIVE DISASTER

WHO IS RESPONSIBLE?

WHY WAS A HOSPITAL CONTAINING RADIOTHERAPY MATERIAL ABANDONED?

PUBLIC OUTRAGE – GOVERNMENT UNDER FIRE

DR MARKANDEYAN EXPLAINS RADIATION SCANDAL

Some channels showed Mark's picture nonstop. The man who saved the river, the man who discovered the truth, the man who now looked like a ghost of himself.

Stella and little Lucy did not survive.

Their bodies, along with others from the colony, were sealed in lead-lined coffins, their funerals conducted quietly under strict radioactive handling protocols. Priests prayed from a distance. The families watched from behind barricades, crying into handkerchiefs, unable even to touch the coffins for a final farewell. Workers poured concrete over each grave. Two layers. Then a third.

Mark attended the burial from afar.

In the capital, the government scrambled. Opposition demanded resignations. Ministers held emergency meetings. The Health Ministry faced national inquiry.

For a month, every news channel in the country fed on the catastrophe like vultures circling a carcass. Reporters stood in front of the hospital ruins with dramatic music in the background. Anchors yelled into microphones.

'Who left a radiotherapy unit abandoned?'

'Who denied the owner access to retrieve hazardous materials?'

'Who allowed a ticking radioactive source to sit for years without inspection?'

When the truth surfaced that the clinic owner had begged for permission to retrieve the cesium but was blocked by judicial red tape and bureaucratic delays the media exploded again. He had committed suicide years ago after being bankrupt. He left a note.

'The red tapes of the judiciary and the government will be responsible for the cesium bomb.'

Dr Mark was hailed a hero.

However, there were some comments under such news in the social media.

'It is all a conspiracy of the medical mafia!'

'Cancer is artificially created by doctors to sell expensive medicines!'

'Dr Mark is the leader of the medical mafia!

CHAPTER NINE
The Cursed Lamp

The old wall clock above the bookshelf ticked with exaggerated clarity. Mark's house, which had witnessed urgency, deception, fear and confrontation in recent days, now felt strangely emptied of tension.

Mark sat on the single-seater armchair near the window. Ashok occupied the sofa opposite him. Neither of them spoke for a long time.

Ashok broke it first.

'So, doc,' he said, attempting a light tone that failed midway, 'does this mean we are going to die early?'

Mark did not look up immediately. His eyes remained fixed outside. He inhaled slowly before replying.

'We are now more vulnerable to cancer,' he said evenly. 'Which means, yes, there is a possibility. Our biological margin has narrowed. One could say our lifeline has been shortened.'

Ashok took it in without speaking. The ticking clock seemed louder now.

'But,' Mark continued, finally turning his gaze towards

him, 'this is not the same as a death sentence. Medical science is improving every day. Detection is better. Treatments are better. Outcomes are better. We might still live long enough to complain about diabetes and cholesterol.'

Ashok let out a faint smile.

'Hmm,' he said. 'Anyway, I am just glad we stopped what we stopped. A mass nuclear disaster. That matters more. Even if we put our own lives on the line.'

Mark replied after a beat. 'Yes. That part matters.'

Ashok leaned back against the sofa. He stretched his legs out.

'I have this feeling,' he said after a moment, 'that this is not the end of it. That we are going to run into more strange things. Especially now that you are getting popular as a paranormal investigator.'

Mark did not respond. He watched Ashok closely instead. The young man looked thinner than he had a year ago. His hairline had receded slightly at the temples. There was a faint shadow beneath his eyes that no amount of sleep ever seemed to erase.

Ashok noticed the silence and turned his head.

Mark shifted in his chair. He straightened slightly with a changing expression. The relaxed mask fell away.

'About that,' Mark said. 'I wanted to tell you something.'

'What is it, doc?' Ashok asked.

Mark folded his hands together.

'I have to let you go,' he said.

The words landed heavily in the room.

Ashok blinked. 'Let me go?'

'Yes.'

'You mean,' Ashok began, then stopped, 'are you firing me?'

Mark did not answer immediately.

'Did I do something wrong?' Ashok continued with slightly rising his voice. 'Did I mess something up? I have always done my best. You know that. I have never refused any work. Driving, research, paperwork, cooking, anything. I have always—'

'That,' Mark interrupted, 'is exactly my problem.'

Ashok stared at him, confused.

'I don't understand,' he said.

Mark leaned forward, resting his elbows on his knees.

'When I hired you,' he said, 'it was supposed to be temporary. You had failed two or three papers in your final semester. The idea was that you would work with me, earn some money, clear those exams and move on.'

Ashok's gaze dropped to the floor.

'Instead,' Mark continued, 'you did not even attempt the exams again. You froze. And now, technically, you are not even a graduate. Which is absurd, because you have the knowledge and skill set of someone who could easily pursue a doctorate.'

Ashok shifted uncomfortably.

'You have become my assistant, my driver, my cook, my errand boy,' Mark said. 'You do everything efficiently. Quietly. Without complaint.'

Ashok opened his mouth to protest, but Mark raised a hand.

'How old are you now?' Mark asked.

Ashok hesitated. 'Twenty-seven. Almost twenty-eight.'

'And what about your life?' Mark asked. 'Your dreams? A stable job? A family? Marriage? A sense of arrival? Are you content being my sidekick forever?'

Ashok's throat tightened. 'I like working with you,' he said softly.

Mark smiled sadly.

'You have found your comfort zone,' he said. 'And comfort

zones are dangerous places for talented people. Artists die in them. Scientists rot in them. Thinkers shrink in them.'

He stood up and began pacing slowly across the room.

'I don't want you to be my sidekick, Ashok, standing behind me like Robin to Batman. That role may look heroic, but it is still living in someone else's shadow. You have the mind and talent to lead your own life, your own cases, to be known for your name, not because you worked for me. If I keep you here, I'm stealing your future. I want you to be a hero on your own, not a supporting character in my story.'

Ashok looked up, startled. 'That is too much,' he said. 'I am just—'

'No,' Mark said firmly. 'You are not just anything. You have an instinct for behavioural patterns that cannot be taught. Your observations during cases are sharper than most trained professionals. Criminal psychology suits you. You see the cracks others miss.'

He stopped in front of Ashok.

'Go back,' Mark said. 'Finish your degree. Take a Master's. Specialise in criminal psychology. You are good at it.'

Ashok shook his head. 'I can't afford that.'

'I know your financial condition,' Mark replied calmly. 'That is the only thing holding you back. And it should not.'

'No,' Ashok said quickly. 'You don't have to pay for me. I don't want charity.'

Mark's eyes hardened.

'This is not charity,' he said. 'This is an investment. In you. You will repay it later, when you can. Slowly. With dignity.'

Ashok fell silent.

'Listen to me,' Mark said, his voice rising for the first time. 'Our days are numbered now. We took risks that most people never even know exist. So do something meaningful with what remains.'

Ashok's eyes glistened.

'Let your name be written somewhere that matters,' Mark continued. 'In research papers. In court judgements. In records that outlast us.'

He pointed towards the door.

'Go,' he said. 'Get out of here.'

Ashok stood up slowly. He bowed his head slightly, a gesture of respect more than farewell, and walked out of the house.

The ticking clock continued, indifferent. Mark stood alone in the living room, staring at the closed door.

*

By eight in the morning, Jerin was usually downstairs.

His mother measured her days by the sound of his footsteps on the stairs, by the way he would call out to her from the dining table. Even on Sundays, even after late nights, Jerin never slept past eight.

That morning, the house stayed quiet.

At nine, his father glanced at the clock and said nothing. At ten, his mother stood near the staircase, listening. The silence felt thicker than usual. She told herself he must be exhausted, that the previous night's editing session had gone on longer than he admitted.

At eleven, worry hardened into fear.

They went upstairs together. Jerin's room was locked from the inside. His mother knocked gently at first, calling his name. No answer. She knocked again, louder. His father tried the handle. It would not move.

'Jerin,' his father called, forcing calm into his voice. 'Open the door.'

There was nothing.

Phones were dialled with shaking fingers. Neighbours gathered in the corridor. Someone suggested forcing the door, someone else said to wait for professionals. The rescue team arrived.

The door gave way with a sound that would haunt the family long after.

Jerin was hanging from the ceiling fan. His body was still and his face strangely peaceful. His mother screamed. His father stood frozen, unable to step forward, unable to step back.

There was no note.

No message.

No explanation.

The police asked questions that led nowhere. Friends stood outside the house in stunned silence, shaking their heads again and again, repeating the same sentence like a prayer that refused to work. Jerin was not that kind of boy. He laughed too easily. He dreamed too loudly. He complained about small things and planned for big ones.

Rumours, as always, arrived faster than understanding.

A secret love affair gone wrong, someone whispered. Financial trouble, said another. Depression hidden behind smiles. But his friends knew him too well for those stories to settle. They searched his phone, his laptop, his notebooks. Nothing pointed towards despair.

At the funeral, his friends spoke of films.

Jerin had been making a short film, something experimental, something he believed would change his life. They talked about locations he had scouted, shots he had planned, arguments he had started over lighting and camera angles. They spoke about how excited he had been in the last few weeks, how he had dragged them to dusty godowns and cluttered shops, looking for the right props.

'He was finally getting everything ready,' one of them said, voice breaking. 'We were just testing the art properties.

Just trying them out.'

'Where do you get all these props from?' a neighbour asked out of curiosity.

'From Saji chettan's art property rentals,' the friend replied.

The neighbour's eyes widened slightly. 'Ah. That shop used to be run by Saji's elder brother, Reji. Poor fellow. He committed suicide last year.'

The sentence lingered.

Someone else leaned in. Someone repeated it. Someone added another detail. Conversations overlapped, then aligned, then spread. From the funeral crowd to the tea shops. From the tea shops to WhatsApp groups. From there to the wider town, the district, the state.

Patterns began to form where grief had left gaps.

Within days, Rashid Parambilmana's video appeared online.

The thumbnail itself was enough to pull people in. A dimly lit room. A red cloth spread carefully over a wooden table. At its centre sat an old kerosene lamp, framed like a relic.

The video opened with Rashid's familiar voice.

'This cursed lamp,' he said, 'will kill anyone who dares to light it.'

The lamp rested on the table once again, demanding attention.

It was not ornate. Not spectacular. It was the kind of object most people had seen in a pre-internet era, forgotten in storerooms, brought out during power cuts and put away again without ceremony. Something that was widely used before electricity was common in Kerala. Yet under the camera's gaze, it appeared different.

The body of the lamp was made of dull brass, darkened by age and use, its surface bearing faint scratches and fingerprints of hands long gone. The oil reservoir sat below, rounded and heavy, with a small hollow column rising through its centre like a spine. This central tube was not decorative. It was purposeful. It channelled air upward, straight into the heart of the flame.

Around that hollow tube sat the wick. Not flat, not simple, but woven into a tube itself, stitched neatly along its length, forming a ring that hugged the inner draft tube. The wick rested between two metal sleeves, inner and outer, held in place by a toothed rack connected to a small wheel. When turned, the mechanism allowed the wick to rise or sink with precise obedience.

It had the necessary holder to place a glass chimney but this one lacked that addition. It was naked. Maybe the glass chimney have been lost in its history. This was a central-draft lamp, a descendant of the Argand lamps of the eighteenth century, designed not for beauty but for efficiency.

Kerosene used to be filled the reservoir below, thinner than the whale oil once used in older lamps, climbing patiently through the wick by capillary action. No gravity-fed drama here. Just quiet physics at work.

Under Rashid's lighting, the lamp looked ancient, almost intelligent, as though it knew how many hands had turned its wheel, how many nights it had pushed back darkness.

Rashid's fingers never touched the wick.

'This lamp,' he continued, 'has a history. A deadly one.'

The video cut to images of Jerin. His smiling photographs. Clips from his unfinished short film. Then to the art property shop, dusty shelves, rows of forgotten objects.

'The latest victim was Jerin, a twenty-one-year-old boy from Kochi,' Rashid said. 'He rented this lamp from an art properties store. That store is now run by Saji. His elder brother, Reji, committed suicide last year.'

The camera returned to the lamp.

'Saji claims that Reji had lit this very lamp when he first acquired it. After that, the lamp sat unused for a year. Until it reached Jerin.'

Rashid paused, letting silence do its work.

'The story does not stop there,' he said. 'Our team tracked three more previous owners. All of them died by suicide after lighting this lamp.'

Comments flooded in faster than the video could buffer. Shock. Fear. Belief. Skepticism drowned beneath repetition.

Rashid leaned closer to the camera.

'Do not worry,' he said. 'I have put a stop to this curse. The lamp is now under my custody. No one else will light it.'

A faint smile touched his lips.

'Unless,' he added softly, 'someone wants to dare to prove its supernatural powers wrong.'

The video ended.

In the days that followed, the internet seemed to lose its grip on reason.

Every timeline, every forwarded message, every late-night discussion spiralled back to the same object. The lamp. Stories multiplied like reflections in broken mirrors. There were no explanations grounded in fact. Only fear dressed up as folklore.

Rashid Parambilmana's video crossed from social media into mainstream news. Debates erupted on television panels where no one had seen the lamp but everyone had an opinion. The word 'curse' was repeated so often it began to sound scientific.

Mark watched it all from a distance.

He sat at the small dining table in his house, a cup of untouched tea cooling beside him, his phone lying face-up. Notifications blinked and faded. He did not open them.

The phone rang.

He glanced at the screen. *Meena.*

'Yes, Meena. Tell me,' Mark said, answering calmly.

Her voice arrived sharp, stripped of pleasantries. 'You are sitting idle while people are drowning in superstition.'

Mark frowned slightly. 'I do not understand.'

'Aren't you aware of this cursed lamp nonsense being promoted by Rashid Parambilmana?' Meena said. 'People are falling for it. You don't have anything to say about it?'

'I have heard about it,' Mark replied. 'But I take up cases only when someone directly approaches me. Victims. Families. Aggrieved parties. The police. In this case, no one has come to me. Not even the family of the boy who died. If they had, I would have investigated and offered an explanation.'

'That is not enough,' Meena said, her frustration rising. 'You are not just another doctor. You know that. People trust you. They listen to you. You have a public responsibility whether you like it or not.'

Mark leaned back in his chair.

'Influence cuts both ways,' he said. 'If I speak without evidence, I become just another voice adding to the noise.'

'And if you stay silent,' Meena snapped, 'you let Rashid control the narrative. You let fear win. You can influence people positively, Mark. Take this case. Give a scientific explanation. Or even prove that the lamp has nothing to do with these deaths and that they are coincidences. People will believe you.'

'How can I take the case when nobody has asked me to?' Mark said. 'I have not even seen the lamp in person.'

There was a brief pause on the line, then Meena spoke again, slower now, almost triumphant.

'Did you miss Rashid's open challenge?'

Mark's eyes narrowed. 'What challenge?'

'He has publicly challenged any skeptic to light the lamp and survive for three days,' Meena said. 'That is apparently the deadline. If you accept the challenge, he will hand over the lamp to you himself.'

Mark exhaled quietly. The word challenge carried a familiar stench. Ego. Spectacle. Theatre disguised as bravery.

'I see,' he said.

'This is exactly what people need,' Meena continued. 'A rational voice stepping into the circus and breaking it from within.'

Mark drummed his fingers lightly against the table. 'Before I do anything, I need to run a background investigation. I need to know whether there is foul play involved. Whether the suicides are connected by something other than coincidence. I will not jump into a public stunt blindly.'

'Do your investigation,' Meena said. 'But I expect you to take a stand. Hold a press conference. Light the lamp in public. Show people that nothing will happen.'

Mark was silent for a moment.

'Alright,' he said finally. 'I will do that. Meanwhile, you organise the press conference. And take custody of the lamp from Rashid Parambilmana.'

Meena did not hide her relief. 'I will contact him immediately.'

The call ended.

Mark placed the phone back on the table and stared at it for a long moment.

Superstition, he knew, did not survive on darkness alone. It survived on silence.

*

Jyolsna arrived at Mark's house just after sunset.

'Thanks a lot, Jyolsna, for investigating the story,' Mark said. He handed her a cup of tea, the steam curling upward.

'Well, it was my need to,' Jyolsna replied. 'If there was something more to it, I wanted to be the one to break it as news.'

They sat facing each other in the living room.

'So,' Mark said, leaning back into the couch, 'tell me the real story behind this so called cursed lamp.'

Jyolsna took a slow sip of tea.

'Alright. This is what I found. Jerin was a wannabe filmmaker. Talented. Ambitious. He had already made a couple of short films before this.'

Her voice softened slightly as she spoke his name.

'Before his death, Jerin and his friends went to Saji's Art Properties Rental store in Kochi.'

The scene unfolded in Mark's mind as she spoke.

The rental store was a cavernous godown filled with the smell of dust and old wood. Racks rose to the ceiling, crammed with objects from borrowed histories. Fake guns lay beside rusted swords. Cracked mirrors leaned against stacks of imitation antique furniture. It was a museum of lies, built for cinema.

'So, what story are you making for your short film?' Saji asked.

'It's a horror story set in an old tharavadu,' Jerin replied, his eyes already scanning the place. 'We found the perfect location. We just need some suitable items to dress the set. The story is set in the early twentieth century.'

'You'll find plenty of suitable items here. Feel free to explore,' Saji said.

Jerin and his friends moved through the aisles, touching objects, lifting them, imagining scenes that did not yet exist. They argued about camera angles and lighting while running their fingers along chipped wood and tarnished metal.

That was when Jerin stopped.

His eyes had locked onto the kerosene lamp resting alone on a shelf. There was no glass chimney. The brass body bore small dents and scratches.

'Wow,' Jerin said softly. 'This looks amazing. The perfect piece for a pre electricity Kerala home.'

He picked it up carefully and shook it. There was a faint sloshing sound.

'I think there's some kerosene left in it as well,' he said, half amused.

Saji glanced at it briefly. 'Old stock. Probably still works. You want it?'

They discussed the rental terms, filled out forms and loaded the items into their vehicle. The lamp went with them without ceremony.

Back home, Jerin sat with his editor friend in his room. The walls were plastered with posters of films he admired. A laptop glowed on the desk.

'Can you add a flame to this lamp in post production?' Jerin asked. 'In case it doesn't work during shooting.'

The editor spun his chair and examined the lamp. 'Sure. That's easy. But you should try lighting it before the shoot. Just to be safe and realistic.'

That evening, Jerin closed his bedroom door. The house was quiet. He struck a match, brought it close to the wick, and lit the lamp.

The flame caught.

Three days later, Jerin was found dead. Hanging. No note. No explanation.

Jyolsna paused.

'So where did Saji get this lamp?' Mark asked quietly.

'That part goes back a year when the store was run by his elder brother Reji,' Jyolsna said. She set the cup down and continued.

Reji had always been on the lookout for old antiques he could buy cheap and rent out later. His hunting grounds were old tharavadus, especially those being sold off quietly due to debt. It was common. Once proud Nair households reduced to selling their inheritance piece by piece.

He heard about such a house in the eastern parts of Ernakulam district.

When Reji arrived, the tharavadu stood like a tired old man. The tiled roof sagged. The wooden floors had cracked and sunk in places. The walls were mottled with mould and fungus, their white long gone.

A young man named Mithun waited at the entrance.

'The house has a buyer,' Mithun said. 'There are some minor items inside you can take for a price. My mother and I will move to the city. It will be easier for me to travel to work.'

'What about your father?' Reji asked.

'He died ten years ago,' Mithun replied. 'Left behind huge debts and loans. People like to judge me for selling the tharavadu, but they do not know the burden he left me with.'

'I'm sorry to hear that,' Reji said. 'If he had lived longer, he might have managed the debts.'

Mithun laughed bitterly. 'No. He committed suicide. Took the easy way out. A selfish person.'

Reji did not respond.

He explored the house, moving slowly through rooms heavy with neglect. He found an old gramophone buried under cloth. A radio with missing knobs. Framed photographs with faces eaten away by time.

In the attic, beneath layers of dust and cobwebs, he found the lamp.

He bought everything.

Back at his godown, as was his habit, Reji decided to check whether the items still worked. Working items fetched higher rental prices.

That night, he lit the lamp using the kerosene still inside.

Three days later, Reji was found dead. Hanging.

'So, did you dig deeper?' Mark asked.

'Yes,' she replied.

Mark straightened slightly. He had learnt to read that tone. It meant the story had roots.

'Mithun's father, Chandraprakash, lived a fairly carefree life in his tharavadu,' Jyolsna began. 'He did not have a regular job. His expenses were met by selling off parcels of land and other ancestral properties bit by bit. Whatever his forefathers had built over generations slowly turned into money that disappeared just as fast.'

Mark had seen many such lives. Old houses standing proud while the men inside them withered.

'That was when Chandraprakash heard that his uncle's properties were being inherited by the uncle's children,' she continued.

'His mother's brother,' Mark said quietly.

'Yes,' Jyolsna said. 'The moment he heard that, something stirred in him. Not greed exactly. More like wounded pride. He believed something that belonged to him by tradition was slipping away.'

Chandraprakash travelled for nearly three hours to reach the house. The road narrowed as it moved away from the town, turning into a ribbon of broken tar lined with coconut palms. By the time he reached, dusk had begun to settle.

The uncle's son, a man in his early forties, stood at the verandah. His face gloomed when he saw Chandraprakash step in.

'You know, we Nairs follow a matrilineal system,' Chandraprakash said after the initial courtesies. 'Properties of a man do not go to his children but to his sister's children.'

'I'm aware of that,' the man replied. 'That was followed in pre Independence India. My father died last year. You did not even call us to ask how we were doing. The house and the lands are being inherited by me and my sister.'

'I don't want to fight or argue,' Chandraprakash said quickly. 'But for the sake of tradition, give me something that belonged to my uncle.'

The room fell silent.

After a long pause, the man opened an old cupboard.

He gave Chandraprakash three things. A silver ring dulled by age. A small elephant sculpture carved from wood. And an old wooden chest, heavy and sturdy, its lock rusted but intact. Inside it were a few forgotten items, wrapped in cloth and time.

Chandraprakash returned home satisfied. It was not about the value. It was about reclaiming something he believed was his by right.

Back in his tharavadu, he examined the items one by one. The ring. The sculpture. Then the chest.

Inside, among old papers and scraps of cloth, lay the kerosene lamp.

'He kept it there for years,' Jyolsna said. 'He did nothing with it.'

Mark imagined the lamp resting in the dark, untouched, gathering silence.

'Then one day,' she continued, 'with nothing else to do, Chandraprakash felt curious. He lit it.'

She paused.

'Three days later, he was found dead. Hanging.'

Mark exhaled slowly.

'So Chandraprakash's uncle also died by suicide?' he asked.

'No,' Jyolsna replied. 'He died naturally. Old age.'

Mark leaned back. 'So the chain ends there.'

Jyolsna shook her head. 'No.'

Mark looked at her sharply.

'His uncle had another son,' she said. 'An elder one. Not the man who argued with Chandraprakash. This son committed suicide in the same house more than thirty years ago.'

Silence spread between them like a stain.

'Tell me,' Mark said.

Jyolsna's voice lowered.

'In the late nineteen eighties, Chandraprakash's uncle Narayanan lived there with his wife and three children. He was a self made man. He wanted a modern life, far away from the traditions he had grown up with in his ancestral tharavadu.'

She described the house as it was then. Tube lights. A black and white television. Battery powered emergency lamps stacked neatly on a shelf.

'Narayanan disliked old things,' she said. 'Everything traditional reminded him of a life he wanted to escape. All the old items he brought from his tharavadu were locked away in a cabinet. Out of sight. Out of use.'

Mark could see it clearly. The cabinet pushed into a corner, ignored.

'His elder son, Shyam, was around eighteen,' Jyolsna continued. 'Curious. Restless. One day, when no one was home, he opened that cabinet.'

Inside, wrapped in cloth, was the lamp.

'He lit it,' she said.

Three days later, Shyam was found hanging in his room.

Mark closed his eyes briefly.

'Did you find out where Narayanan got this lamp?' he asked.

'From his mother's tharavadu,' Jyolsna replied. 'I went there to learn more. But the place is gone. The house has been demolished. There were no leads to trace further back.'

Mark stared at the floor.

'It must be hundred years old,' he said.

'Yes,' Jyolsna replied. 'At least.'

Mark lifted his head slowly.

'So the stories were right,' he said. 'Everyone who lit the lamp committed suicide. No external force involved.'

'Yes,' Jyolsna said.

Mark stood up and walked towards the window.

'People will say this proves the curse,' he said softly.

'And they will believe it,' Jyolsna said.

Mark turned back to her.

'Patterns do not mean causation,' he said. 'But patterns are enough to terrify people.'

He paused.

'Which means it is now my job to prove that the lamp is not cursed,' he said. 'By lighting it myself and staying alive.'

Jyolsna looked at him, alarm flashing across her face.

'You are serious.'

'Completely,' Mark replied.

He looked calm, almost detached, but his eyes burned with quiet resolve.

'Fear feeds on silence,' he said. 'If I stay quiet, Rashid's story becomes the truth. Someone has to break the chain.'

Jyolsna swallowed. 'And if people are right?'

Mark smiled faintly.

'Then I will die knowing I did not run from fear,' he said. 'But I am not planning to die.'

*

'Rashid won't give us the lamp,' Meena said the moment Mark answered. Her voice was irritated by the negotiation she had clearly lost.

'On what grounds?' Mark asked.

'He says lighting the lamp in a press conference will cause panic,' Meena replied. 'According to him, it will affect the people attending and could even lead to a massacre. He insists that, like all the previous victims, you have to light it alone, inside a closed room.'

'Then how will anyone know whether I actually lit it or not?' he asked.

'He has invited us to his abode,' Meena said. 'He will gather the press there. The lamp will be kept in a closed room with a camera inside. The footage will be telecast live on his YouTube channel. After meeting the media, you will be asked to go in alone and light it.'

Mark leaned back. The arrangement was theatrical, calculated to preserve Rashid's narrative while pretending transparency. Exactly the kind of spectacle Rashid thrived on.

'Okay,' Mark said finally. 'Agreed.'

Meena hesitated. 'You are too calm about this.'

'Fear needs an audience,' Mark replied. 'Let him have one.'

The journey to Alappuzha began the next morning. The car cut through narrow roads lined with canals. Coconut trees leaned inward as though eavesdropping. Meena sat in the front seat, scrolling through her phone. Jyolsna watched the scenery quietly, her journalist's mind assembling headlines even before the event had begun.

Rashid Parambilmana's abode stood apart from the surrounding houses, an old ancestral structure polished into mystique. Green flags fluttered near the gate. By the time they arrived, the courtyard was already crowded. Camera tripods stood like metallic insects, legs spread wide, lenses fixed on the entrance.

As Mark stepped out of the car, a ripple passed through the gathered crowd. Whispers followed him.

Inside, Rashid moved like a host who owned not just

the house but the moment itself. He wore a dark kurta. The cursed lamp was not yet visible, but its presence was felt, spoken about in hushed tones.

Rashid raised his hand and the journalists fell silent.

'I appreciate and acknowledge Dr Markandeyan's attempt to prove the supernatural wrong,' he said, his voice smooth, rehearsed. 'It takes courage to walk into danger knowingly.'

Cameras zoomed in. Red lights blinked on.

Rashid turned slightly toward Mark, his expression softening into something that resembled concern. 'But for the last time, I am advising you, doctor. You do not have to do this. You should live longer and cure people through your medical profession. Why risk your life for this?'

A murmur spread through the press. The words were perfectly chosen. Rashid was not challenging Mark. He was appearing to protect him.

All microphones turned as one toward Mark.

Mark stepped forward. He felt the weight of the moment settle on his shoulders, not as fear, but as responsibility. He glanced briefly at the journalists, then at Rashid and finally at the unseen room where the lamp waited. His face showed no bravado. No theatrical defiance. Only quiet certainty.

'I understand your concern,' he said calmly. 'But fear thrives when left unchallenged.'

The room leaned closer, hungry for every word.

Mark stepped closer to the microphones. The murmurs died down. He did not raise his voice, yet it carried.

'I accepted this challenge because fear spreads faster than truth,' he said. 'When people cannot explain something, they wrap it in the language of curses, gods or demons. That fear then begins to dictate their choices, their mental health and sometimes their deaths. As a doctor and as a human being, I cannot watch that silently.'

He looked briefly at Rashid, then back at the cameras.

'I am certain there is nothing paranormal about this lamp because every so called pattern has a human explanation. Psychological vulnerability, coincidence, suggestion and social contagion are far more powerful than any invisible force. When people are told again and again that something will kill them, some minds comply. That is not magic. That is conditioning.'

A pause.

'I am here to draw a clear line between belief and evidence. If I light this lamp and live, it will not be because I am special or protected. It will be because the lamp has no power at all.'

His voice toughened slightly.

'I am confident I will live well beyond a week because kerosene lamps do not kill people. Fear does. And tonight, I intend to prove that fear wrong.'

CHAPTER TEN

After the Flame

Rashid opened the door and stepped aside. Mark entered without hesitation.

The room swallowed him whole.

A single tungsten bulb hung from the ceiling. The walls were bare, unpainted concrete, stained with damp shadows. There were no windows. No vents. No fans. The air felt sealed, thick with the stale odour of dust.

Behind him, outside the door, rose the muffled noise of voices. Journalists clearing throats. Camera shutters. Someone coughing. People breathing in anticipation.

The door closed.

The click of the latch echoed louder than it should have.

For a brief second, Mark stood still, letting his eyes adjust. He noticed the cameras next. Three of them. One fixed high in the corner, its wide lens capturing the entire room. Another positioned directly toward the small wooden table at the centre. The third pointed at him, unblinking, red recording light glowing faintly like a watching eye.

He knew exactly what Rashid was doing. No gaps. No doubts. No room for claims of trickery.

Mark walked towards the table, his footsteps dull against the concrete floor. The table was old, its surface scratched and uneven, with a faint burn mark near one leg. On top of it sat the lamp.

A kerosene lamp. Brass. Darkened by age. The metal base bore tiny dents and scratches, signs of a long, careless life passed through many hands. It looked disappointingly ordinary.

Beside it lay a matchbox.

Mark exhaled quietly through his nose. He had expected something theatrical. Symbols. Runes. Something designed to unsettle the mind. Instead, this was just an object. Old. Forgotten. Misunderstood.

'Let's get this over with,' he murmured, more to himself than the cameras.

He picked up the matchbox, shook it once and slid it open. The rasp of the match striking the strip sounded violent in the silence. The flame flared to life, sharp and blue at its base, yellow at the tip.

He bent forward and touched it to the wick. Thick black smoke burst upward before thinning into a wavering plume. The wick glowed orange, then settled, casting a weak but steady light that barely challenged the tungsten bulb above. The smell of burning kerosene spread through the room, heavy and acrid.

Mark straightened and stepped back.

Five minutes, Rashid had said. No more. No less.

He stood there, hands loosely at his sides, eyes occasionally drifting to the camera that watched him most closely. The seconds dragged. The heat from the lamp prickled faintly against his skin.

Nothing happened.

No whisper. No movement. No sense of unease beyond the mild irritation of the smoke scratching his throat.

After what felt like far longer than five minutes, Mark reached forward and blew gently. The flame flickered, resisted for a second, then died with a thin curl of smoke rising from the wick.

The room fell back into its earlier stillness.

Almost immediately, the door opened.

Fresh air rushed in like a relief. Rashid stood outside, his expression carefully neutral. Mark stepped out, blinking as the noise of the press flooded his ears all at once.

Cameras surged forward. Microphones crowded his face.

Meena was there instantly, gripping his hand firmly, her fingers warm and grounding. Jyolsna stood just behind her, eyes searching his face for any sign of distress.

'I will now appear again on the fourth day and tell you the lamp is not cursed,' Mark said clearly, his voice steady. 'There is nothing paranormal here.'

A few claps broke out. Hesitant at first, then louder.

Rashid folded his hands, his voice solemn. 'I will pray for your safety, doctor.'

Mark offered a polite response. He felt only tired.

They left soon after. The car rolled away from Rashid Parambilmana's house and merged onto the highway toward Thiruvananthapuram. Evening had deepened into night.

Inside the car, the tension dissolved quickly. Jyolsna joked about how the media would spin the event. Meena drifted into a rant about recent elections and empty promises. Mark listened, occasionally responding, his hands steady on the steering wheel.

The fatigue crept in slowly.

Not sleepiness. Something heavier. A dull pressure behind his eyes.

'Long day,' Meena said, noticing his silence.

'Yes,' Mark replied. 'Just need rest.'

The road stretched ahead, dark and familiar. Then, on the left side of the road, he saw her.

A young woman.

She stood just beyond the shoulder, cradling an infant against her chest. She wasn't moving. Just standing there, her face turned slightly away from the headlights.

Mark slowed instinctively.

His fingers tightened on the wheel.

'Careful,' he muttered.

The woman did not step onto the road. The car passed without incident.

'What?' Jyolsna asked.

'Nothing,' Mark said. 'Just someone by the roadside.'

They drove on.

Fifteen minutes later, she was there again.

Same posture. Same infant. Same stillness.

Mark frowned. His mind reached for explanations. Fatigue. Pattern recognition. Coincidence.

He did not slow this time.

Another thirty minutes passed.

The conversation had drifted into silence. The hum of the engine filled the car. Then, suddenly, the headlights caught movement.

She was directly ahead.

This time, she stepped onto the road.

Mark's heart slammed against his ribs.

Her face turned fully toward him.

Saranya.

His wife.

The infant in her arms was wrapped in white cloth. Her eyes were fixed on him with an expression that was neither accusation nor sorrow.

'No,' Mark whispered.

His foot slammed the brake.

The car screeched violently. Tyres shrieked as it skidded to a stop. Jyolsna was thrown forward, screaming. Meena grabbed the dashboard, her shout sharp and panicked.

'What! What happened?' Meena cried. 'Why did you stop?'

Mark sat frozen, chest heaving, hands still locked around the steering wheel. His breath came in ragged gasps.

'There was someone on the road,' he said.

They looked ahead.

The road was empty.

No woman. No infant. No trace of movement.

Meena turned to him slowly. 'Mark… you're exhausted.'

Mark's throat tightened, dry and raw.

Meena placed a hand on his arm. 'You need rest. Let me drive.'

Mark did not argue.

He stepped out of the car. His legs felt unsteady as he walked around to the passenger side. Meena took the driver's seat and pulled back onto the road.

As the car moved forward, Mark settled his head against the window, watching the darkness slide past.

Viswamitran arrived after nightfall. The garden lamps along Mark's walkway glowed dimly. Mark was in the study, sorting through notes, when the doorbell rang.

He opened the door to find his brother standing there with a cloth bag in his hand. The smell of home-cooked food escaped through the folds.

'I have brought you dinner,' Viswamitran said.

Mark stepped aside and let him in. 'Thanks.'

They moved into the dining area. Viswamitran placed the containers on the table but did not open them. He stood there with stiff shoulders.

'Why did you accept that challenge?' he asked finally.

Mark paused, then sat down. 'It was necessary,' he said calmly. 'Don't worry, brother. This doesn't involve vile politicians or the mafia. I'm safe.'

Viswamitran shook his head, frustration tightening his jaw. 'Lighting a cursed lamp that supposedly drives people to suicide. That's worse. There was no need for you to do that.'

Mark smiled faintly, the expression tired rather than amused. 'Relax. There are no cursed lamps. And I'm not going to kill myself.'

Viswamitran did not return the smile. His gaze drifted around the house. The lights were on, but the rooms felt empty, too quiet.

'Where is Ashok?' he asked. 'I didn't see him in the news with you.'

'I let him go,' Mark replied. 'The guy needs to finish his education.'

Viswamitran frowned. 'So you're alone here?'

'Apparently, yes,' Mark said. 'Like most times.'

There was a brief silence.

'Come sleep at my place,' Viswamitran said.

Mark shook his head. 'All my books and work stuff are here.'

Viswamitran exhaled sharply. 'Then I'll sleep here tonight. And for the next three days.'

Mark chuckled, though there was no humour in it. 'Oh, brother, please. You're still worried about that curse nonsense. I'll be okay. Go back home and sleep peacefully.'

They talked for another hour, circling familiar topics.

Work. Family. Things neither of them truly wanted to say. When Viswamitran finally rose to leave, Mark walked him to the door.

Viswamitran hesitated at the doorstep. Then he turned back.

'You know,' he said quietly, 'you don't have to be alone like this. You can still marry someone.'

Mark's face hardened as the faint warmth drained from his eyes.

'No one will replace Saranya,' he said.

He closed the door with firm care, without waiting for a reply.

Sleep came to Mark like a slow tide, heavy and irresistible that night. When his mind finally slipped under, it did not fall into the usual blackness. Instead, images bloomed with unsettling precision.

It felt like a dream, yet sharper. Too coherent. Too alive.

Mark found himself standing on a familiar college pathway. He knew this place. The benches. The chipped red tiles.

Saranya was beside him.

She looked exactly as she had then. Younger. Carefree. Her hair tied loosely, a few strands falling across her forehead. She was smiling, that effortless smile that had once anchored his entire world.

They walked together, shoulders brushing, fingers occasionally touching and retreating with shy delight. They sat on park benches, shared cheap coffee in crowded cafés, whispered jokes in the darkness of cinema halls while others hissed at them to be quiet. Time folded easily around them.

Mark felt light. Whole.

The dream shifted, smoothly, like turning a page.

They were no longer in the same city. He saw himself

typing messages on an old phone, waiting for replies late into the night. He heard her voice through crackling phone calls, distances collapsing for a few stolen minutes. Sometimes there were long online chats through computers, words piling up faster than sleep could claim them.

Different states. Different lives. And yet, always the same certainty.

There were only a handful of days each year when they could be together. Train journeys counted down in anticipation. Brief reunions that felt like festivals compressed into hours. And always, the ache of parting.

Their relationship had never been hidden. Their families knew. There were no dramatic confrontations, no forbidden meetings. Just patience. A shared understanding that life required structure before surrender.

They had promised themselves not to rush. Degrees first. Jobs. Stability.

For that, they waited.

Mark watched years pass like gentle dissolves. He saw himself land his first job, the pride mixed with exhaustion. Saranya was still studying then, buried in textbooks with her dreams intact. When she finally finished, there was another delay. Her elder sister's marriage had to come first. Customs. Responsibilities. Family rhythms that could not be disrupted.

Still, they waited.

And it was worth it.

He saw them sitting together one evening, older now, hands entwined, the future no longer abstract.

'We will live and love together till the end,' Mark heard himself say. 'Till we die together.'

Saranya laughed softly, her eyes luminous. 'Or maybe in the afterlife too. Maybe in our next life, we will be together again.'

Mark smiled, the familiar skepticism rising naturally. 'Gotta break it to you. There are no next lives. We have to make the maximum of this one.'

She nestled against him, unoffended, content.

The scene shifted again.

Wedding lights. Familiar faces. A quiet ceremony filled with relief more than spectacle. Years of waiting had distilled the moment into something pure. When he held her then, it felt earned. Solid. Real.

'Finally,' he whispered into her hair. 'Now I can start my life with you.'

He hugged her tightly.

And then he felt it.

Pain.

Sudden. Sharp. Scorching.

Heat surged against his chest. He pulled back instinctively, confusion flaring into terror. Saranya was burning. Flames licked up her arms, consumed her sari, reflected wildly in her eyes. She did not scream. She only looked at him, expression frozen between surprise and sorrow.

'Saranya,' he cried, reaching out.

His hands passed through fire. Her body collapsed inward, breaking apart, turning to ash that scattered at his feet.

Mark screamed.

His eyes flew open.

Morning light flooded the room, harsh. His breath came in ragged gasps, his body drenched in sweat.

It was the next day.

Mark reported to the hospital for his consulting duty with a heaviness that clung to him like an anvil. The long sleep from the previous night had done nothing to restore him. His body moved through routine out of habit, but his mind lagged behind, dull and bruised.

Mark sat behind his desk in the consultation room. One patient after another entered, spoke, wept, argued, or sat in silence. He listened. He diagnosed. He prescribed. His voice remained calm, measured, reassuring.

Between consultations, the medical assistant guide patients to the laboratory or the pharmacy. When she stepped out with one such patient, the room fell quiet.

Mark was alone.

The door opened again.

A young woman entered and closed it softly behind her. Her steps were slow, hesitant. She sat on the chair opposite Mark, her head bowed, hair falling forward like a curtain. Her face was not revealed.

Mark straightened in his chair.

'What seems to be the problem, miss?' he asked politely.

No reply.

Her hands rested on her lap, fingers tightly intertwined. She did not lift her face.

Mark waited. Silence was not unfamiliar territory for him. Many patients struggled to find words. Some took minutes. Some never spoke at all. But usually, there was someone with them. A parent. A spouse. A friend.

This woman was alone.

'Miss,' Mark said again, his tone soft but firmer. 'You can take your time. But you need to tell me what brings you here.'

Nothing.

A faint unease crept into his chest. He glanced toward the door, expecting the medical assistant to return any moment.

Mark stood up slowly, the chair scraping faintly against the floor. He took a step closer to the woman, careful not to startle her.

'If you're uncomfortable,' he said, lowering himself slightly to meet her line of sight, 'you can wait outside until the assistant comes back.'

For a moment, nothing changed.

Then the woman lifted her head.

Mark's breath caught violently.

It was Saranya.

Her eyes looked exactly as they had in his dream. Deep. Familiar. Unbearably real.

Mark staggered back as if struck. His heel caught the leg of the chair behind him and he fell hard to the floor.

At that exact moment, the door burst open.

The medical assistant rushed in, alarm flashing across her face. She dropped the files in her hand and hurried toward him.

'Doctor!' she cried, grabbing his arm. 'What happened?'

Mark stared past her, his heart pounding wildly.

The chair opposite him was empty.

There was no woman. No bowed head. No familiar face.

The assistant helped him up, steadying him as he reclined against the desk.

'Are you alright?' she asked, her voice tight with concern.

'Yes,' he said after a moment. His voice sounded distant, even to his own ears. 'I slipped.'

She frowned but said nothing, still watching him closely.

'Call the next patient,' he said.

The assistant hesitated, then turned and stepped back outside.

Mark lowered himself into his chair. His hands trembled just enough that he had to clasp them together to hide it. His gaze lingered on the empty space where the woman had sat.

The room felt colder now.

That night, Mark decided he had earned the right to rest. The day had scraped him raw and his mind felt bruised in ways he could not name. He ordered dinner through an app, choosing something familiar, something that required no thought. When the food arrived, he ate mechanically, barely tasting it and then settled onto the couch.

He switched on the television and scrolled through the streaming platform with deliberate care. No thrillers. No mysteries. No documentaries that might spiral into dread. He chose a comedy, bright poster, smiling faces, harmless nonsense. Laughter, he told himself, was medicine.

The film began. Colours flashed. Jokes landed. Mark found himself smiling, then laughing, a real laugh that loosened something tight in his chest. For a while, the world narrowed to punchlines and exaggerated reactions. He shifted back, comforted by the predictability of it all.

Then, faintly, a sound crept in.

A baby crying.

Mark frowned. In the scene on screen, characters were talking in a crowded room. Somewhere in the background, an infant wailed. He assumed it was part of the film. The scene cut to another location, a brightly lit office.

The crying continued.

Mark sat up straighter. His eyes darted to the speakers, then to the screen. The characters were laughing. No baby in sight.

The crying grew sharper, more insistent.

Mark grabbed the remote and paused the movie.

The screen froze.

The crying did not.

His breath quickened. The sound was no longer distant or muffled. It felt closer, as though it was coming from inside the house, seeping through the walls.

'No,' he whispered.

His thumb trembled as he switched off the television.

Silence.

The crying stopped instantly, as if someone had cut a wire.

Mark exhaled slowly with his heart thudding. He ran a hand through his hair and let out a nervous chuckle. He switched the television back on. The comedy resumed. The jokes still worked. He laughed again, louder this time, as if to prove something to himself. He needed this. He deserved a few minutes of normalcy.

When the film ended, the house felt quieter than before. Mark turned off the lights and went to bed.

Sleep, however, refused to come.

He lay on his back, staring at the ceiling fan as it spun in steady circles, its shadow slicing the room into rotating patterns. His thoughts drifted without direction. Faces. Voices. Memories. He closed his eyes. Opened them. Shifted position. Nothing helped.

His body was exhausted. His mind would not follow.

Finally, he closed his eyes again.

When he opened them, the ceiling fan was gone.

Above him stretched a canopy of leaves, dense and alive, sunlight slipping through in pale shards. The air was cool and damp, heavy with the smell of earth and moss.

Mark tried to sit up.

He couldn't.

A strange panic rose in him. He tried to move his arms. There were none. He tried to stand straight, but his body would not obey. His balance felt wrong, tilted forward.

He looked down.

Four legs.

Slender. Powerful. Covered in coarse brown fur.

'What…' he tried to say.

No words came.

Instinct took over. He moved, running through the forest with a grace that did not belong to a human body. Trees blurred past. The ground felt alive beneath his hooves. Fear mixed with exhilaration in a way he had never known.

A lake appeared ahead, its surface smooth and dark. Thirst burned in him. He lowered his head and drank.

As the water rippled, his reflection stared back.

Antlers. Wide, branching. A stag.

He froze.

Footsteps rustled behind him. Soft. Familiar.

He turned.

A female deer stood a few paces away, her eyes calm, knowing.

'Mark, it's me,' she said.

His heart surged.

'Saranya?' he asked, though the sound was not speech but understanding.

'Yes,' she replied, stepping closer. 'Didn't I tell you we would be together in our next life as well. Somehow, we both became deer in this one.'

They moved toward each other, heads lowering, antlers and forehead touching lightly. The forest around them felt safe, hushed, as if holding its breath. They lay down beside the lake, bodies pressed close, warmth shared under the stars.

Peace settled over him.

Mark opened his eyes. It was daylight. The next day.

The ceiling fan rotated above him, unchanged, indifferent. His arms were back. His legs were human.

He lay there, breathing hard, the echo of hooves and moonlight still clinging to him.

The rain had been falling since dawn, but by midmorning it had thickened into something heavier, angrier. Clouds pressed low over Thiruvananthapuram, swallowing the city in a bruised, metallic gloom. Sheets of rain lashed against Mark's windows and thunder rolled so close it rattled the glass panes in their frames. Lightning tore open the sky again and again, white and violent, followed by crashes that made the house shudder.

The power went off with a dull click.

Mark stood in the middle of the living room for a moment, listening. The ceiling fan slowed to a stop. The refrigerator fell silent. Only the rain remained, relentless, pounding the roof like fists.

He did not switch on the inverter.

He wanted the darkness.

Though it was still daytime, the house felt submerged in night. Shadows pooled in corners. The staircase vanished into a grey blur. Mark had eaten little that morning, just a dry sandwich that sat uneasily in his stomach. Hunger felt irrelevant now. His body was tired in a way sleep could not touch.

The storm's noise pressed in on him. He tried to read. He tried to paint. He tried to sit still. Nothing held his attention. His thoughts slid and collided.

Then he heard it.

'Mark…'

The voice was soft, female, familiar enough to make his breath catch.

He froze.

The house was empty. He knew that. He had locked the doors himself. Still, his heart began to pound.

'Mark… dear… come to me.'

The voice drifted again, clearer now, coming from upstairs.

His legs moved before his mind could argue. He crossed the living room and climbed the staircase slowly. The rain roared outside, thunder cracking so loudly it felt like it split the walls.

He reached the bedroom.

She was standing there.

Saranya.

She looked exactly as she had in life. Hair loose around her shoulders. The faint mole near her collarbone. The eyes that had once held laughter, patience, love. She smiled at him, softly.

'Mark… I missed you,' she said.

Something inside him broke.

'I missed you too,' he sobbed, crossing the room in two steps. He wrapped his arms around her, burying his face against her shoulder. She felt warm. Real. Solid.

For a moment, the world made sense again.

Then she pulled back slightly and looked at him.

'Why did you do it?' she asked.

The question cut through him like ice.

'Did what?' Mark asked.

The room shifted.

The walls stretched and dissolved. The bed vanished. The smell of rain was replaced by antiseptic. Bright lights burned overhead. Mark found himself running down a hospital corridor, his shoes slipping on polished tiles.

'Tell me what happened!' he shouted at a nurse rushing past.

She stopped with tense face.

'It's a complicated pregnancy,' she said. 'Our doctors are doing their best.'

His chest tightened.

'Can I come in?' he asked.

She hesitated, then said, 'Okay.'

He pushed through the swinging doors into the labour room.

Saranya lay on the operating table, her face twisted in agony, sweat plastering her hair to her forehead. Her screams tore through the room, raw and desperate. Doctors and nurses surrounded her, voices sharp and urgent, instruments clinking, monitors beeping in frantic rhythms.

Mark stood frozen near the wall, useless with trembling hands.

'Just breathe… hold on,' a doctor shouted.

Her body convulsed. The screams rose higher, then broke into sobs.

Mark wanted to move. To help. To do something. He could not.

Metal flashed. Blood stained gloves. Mark's vision blurred.

Then he heard it.

A baby's cry.

Sharp. Piercing. Alive.

Relief surged through him so violently he nearly collapsed.

But another sound had stopped.

Saranya was no longer screaming.

The room fell into a terrible stillness beneath the crying infant.

A nurse guided Mark toward the door. 'We will call you,' she said firmly.

He stumbled back into the corridor. Saranya's parents stood there, pale and shaking.

Minutes stretched into an eternity.

Then a doctor emerged.

'I'm sorry,' he said quietly. 'We weren't able to save her. The baby is healthy and under care.'

The words crushed Mark flat.

The world tilted. Darkness rushed over him.

When he woke, he was lying on a narrow bystander's bed in a hospital ward. An IV drip was taped to his arm. Viswamitran sat nearby, his face drawn.

'You fell unconscious,' Viswamitran said softly. 'They

brought you here.'

'Where is Saranya?' Mark asked.

Viswamitran did not answer.

Mark ripped the IV line from his arm and stood up, swaying. His legs barely responded.

'Sit down,' Viswamitran urged. 'You need rest. I'll bring you something to eat. The baby is fine. Look after your child. Saranya's parents are with the doctor.'

He left the room.

Mark's eyes drifted to the crib near the bed.

The baby slept peacefully, tiny chest rising and falling.

Something dark and violent surged through him.

He walked toward the crib. He stayed there for few minutes. He glared at the baby with utmost contempt.

'You… you killed my wife,' he muttered.

He picked up the pillow from the bed.

Pressed it down.

Hard.

He held it there, his arms locked, his jaw clenched, his mind screaming and empty all at once. Five minutes passed. Or maybe five lifetimes.

When he lifted the pillow, the baby lay still.

Mark returned to the bed. He reconnected the IV line with shaking hands and closed his eyes.

Later, voices flooded the room. Nurses. Saranya's parents. Viswamitran.

He heard gasps. Screams. Wailing.

Days blurred together.

Saranya's body lay ready for cremation. Rituals were performed. Incense burned. Prayers murmured. Mark stood numb as flames consumed her body.

'I understand your pain,' a friend whispered beside him. 'Losing your wife and your child. The doctor said the baby was healthy at the time of delivery. Even they don't know what happened… but maybe God knows.'

Mark stared at the fire.

The flames roared higher.

And suddenly, he was back in his bedroom.

Saranya stood before him, burning.

'You killed my child, Mark,' she said, her voice echoing through the crackle of flames.

'I'm sorry,' he whispered. 'I was angry.'

'You're a criminal,' she said. 'A murderer.'

Her body collapsed into ash at his feet.

Mark stood alone again.

Outside, the storm raged on, thunder shaking the house, rain pounding the roof, as the darkness pressed in around him.

Mark stood alone in the bedroom, the storm still muttering outside like a restless conscience.

He opened the cupboard and took out a rope. It felt rough in his hands, heavier than it should have been, as if it already carried weight. He spread it once on the bed, smoothing it with slow, deliberate movements, the way a man might prepare something sacred or final.

He dragged the wooden stool closer and placed it carefully on the mattress. The bed dipped under the weight, springs sighing softly. He climbed up and reached for the ceiling fan. His fingers trembled only slightly as he looped one end of the rope around the metal rod, knotting it tight. He tested it once, twice. It held.

At the other end, he fashioned a crude noose. Not elegant, not theatrical. Just functional. Enough.

Mark stepped down and looked at it.

For a long moment, he simply stood there, breathing slowly, listening to the rain hammering the roof. His reflection stared back at him from the darkened mirror, eyes hollow, face drawn, a stranger wearing his skin.

'This is fair,' he whispered to the empty room. 'This is what I deserve.'

Criminal. Murderer. The words pressed against his skull with merciless clarity. No superstition. No curse. Just consequence.

He climbed back onto the bed and stool. The rope brushed his cheek as he guided the loop over his head. The rope tightened against his throat. He adjusted it carefully, ensuring there would be no escape, no mistake. Everything was precise. Controlled.

He closed his eyes.

Images flickered behind his lids. Saranya's smile. Her voice. The baby's cry. The weight of the pillow in his hands.

Then another thought cut through the fog.

People would talk.

They would say the lamp killed him. That the curse claimed another victim. Fear would grow. Rashid would be proven right. Superstition would win.

That was not the truth.

'I am not dying because of a lamp,' Mark said aloud, his voice hoarse. 'I am dying because of what I did.'

And that was exactly why he could not do this.

To die now would be to lie. To let fear replace responsibility. To allow his guilt to become fuel for madness.

A sharp breath escaped him.

Slowly, deliberately, he loosened the rope from his neck. The pressure eased. Air rushed back into his lungs, burning, humiliating, alive. He lifted the loop away and let it fall limp against his chest.

He stepped down from the stool, his legs unsteady. The bed creaked as he climbed off. With shaking hands, he untied the knot from the fan and gathered the rope.

Mark sank onto the edge of the bed and covered his face.

Outside, thunder rolled again, but it sounded farther away now.

'I won't let my death become another lie,' he whispered.

*

The Janamaithri Police Station crouched under the rain like a weary animal. A car cut through the downpour, headlights blazing unnaturally bright against the rainy darkness of the day. It rolled into the compound and stopped abruptly.

The constables at the front desk straightened at once.

'Who would come at a time like this?' one of them muttered, peering through the glass smeared with rain. 'Must be some higher official.'

No ordinary civilian would come to the police station at weather like this.

The driver's door opened.

Dr Markandeyan stepped out.

Rain soaked him instantly. His hair plastered itself to his forehead. His shirt clung to his body, darkened and heavy. He did not bother to run. He walked steadily through the rain.

'Sir,' he said calmly, his voice steady despite the storm roaring behind him, 'I want to see the SI.'

The constables exchanged looks. One of them recognised him at once.

'Doctor…' the officer said, startled. 'Please come.'

They led him down the narrow corridor, wanted criminals' posters and framed notices curled at the edges from years of humidity. The Sub Inspector looked up as Mark entered.

He froze for a fraction of a second.

'Doctor?' the SI said. 'What brings you here at this odd hour?'

Mark stood in the centre of the room. Water dripped

from his sleeves onto the cracked floor tiles. His eyes were bloodshot.

'You have to arrest me,' Mark said.

The SI blinked.

'I did a murder.'

The words hung in the room like smoke.

The SI stared at him, waiting for laughter, for explanation, for anything that would make sense. Nothing came.

'Doctor,' he said slowly, choosing each word with care, 'tell me where the victim is. If it has just happened, we might still be able to save them.'

Mark shook his head.

'It happened ten years ago,' he replied. 'I killed my infant child.'

Silence settled across the room.

The rain outside seemed to grow louder, hammering the walls, as if trying to break in.

The SI sat down heavily.

An infant. Ten years ago. Murder. Confession. From a man he knew, respected, trusted.

'Doctor,' the SI said at last, his voice low, 'you stay here.'

Mark gave a faint response and sank into the chair opposite the desk, the strength draining out of him all at once.

The SI stepped out of the room, closing the door behind him. He pulled out his phone and dialled a number he rarely used lightly. It was Vikram IPS, the City Commissioner.

'Sir,' he said when the call connected, rain and static crackling through the line, 'it's me. Dr Markandeyan has come to the station. He is confessing to a murder.'

A pause.

'Yes, sir. He says it happened ten years ago. His infant child.'

Another pause, longer this time.

'He is here.'

The SI ended the call and took a deep breath before returning to his room.

He opened the door.

Mark was no longer sitting upright.

He had slumped sideways in the chair, his head tilted back, eyes half-open, breath shallow. Water pooled beneath him from his clothes, spreading slowly across the floor like a dark stain.

'Doctor!' the SI shouted, rushing forward.

Mark did not respond. He was unconscious.

*

Mark opened his eyes slowly. The first thing he felt was the cold pinch in his arm.

A hospital.

He turned his head slightly. Transparent tube ran from his arm to an IV stand beside the bed. The white ceiling above him felt too bright, too close. His body was heavy, uncooperative, as though it did not entirely belong to him.

He was not alone.

Viswamitran stood near the window. Jyolsna stood near the door. Meena rested against the wall. Vikram IPS stood upright near the foot of the bed, hands clasped behind his back. Ashok stood closest to Mark, unmoving, as if afraid that even breathing too loudly might disturb him.

Mark said nothing.

His eyes moved slowly across their faces, registering them without acknowledgement. His mind felt fractured, pieces floating without connection. He needed silence. He needed time.

Ashok glanced at the nurse, who was preparing a syringe and adjusting the IV line.

'How is he, sister?' Ashok asked softly.

The nurse checked Mark's pulse, glanced at the monitor, then gave a small nod. 'He is stable now. You can talk to him. Just keep him calm.'

She finished her work and left the room quietly.

Vikram stepped forward.

'Dr Mark,' he said softly, lowering his voice despite his uniformed authority. 'Do you remember what happened? Why you went to the station?'

Mark swallowed.

'I went to get myself arrested,' he muttered. 'I committed a crime.'

A faint stir passed through the room.

'I know,' Vikram said. 'You collapsed at the station. They brought you here immediately. I was informed and your friends were called.'

He paused, studying Mark's face carefully.

'While you were unconscious, I ordered an investigation. Immediately. Off the records.'

Everyone straightened. Meena's breath caught. Viswamitran turned away from the window.

'My team contacted the doctors,' Vikram continued. 'They visited the hospital where your wife was admitted ten years ago. Labour records, medical notes, witness statements. Everything.'

Mark's eyes flickered.

'You did not kill your child,' Vikram said firmly.

The words landed softly, yet shook the room.

Ashok's eyes widened. Jyolsna covered her mouth.

'The infant was stillborn,' Vikram went on. 'The baby had already died before your wife passed away. Multiple doctors testified to it including your brother. It is on record.'

Mark's breathing grew uneven.

'I don't know why,' Vikram said, his tone thoughtful now,

'but somewhere in your mind, that truth got rewritten. You carried a false memory.'

Mark closed his eyes.

'False memory,' he whispered.

'Yes,' Vikram said.

Mark opened his eyes again. This time, there was clarity in them. A slow, terrifying clarity. Images flashed through his mind. Pieces clicked into place.

He let out a shaky laugh, halfway between relief and horror.

'That's it,' Mark said suddenly, his voice rising. 'That's the answer.'

Everyone froze.

'I found it,' he said, pushing himself slightly upright despite Ashok's instinctive move to hold him down. 'I found the mystery of the cursed lamp.'

They stared at him, stunned.

Rain lashed against the hospital windows outside, as thunder rolled across the city.

*

The press conference hall in Thiruvananthapuram was packed well beyond capacity. Rows of chairs were filled with journalists, camera operators, bloggers and independent streamers, all craning their necks towards the stage. Camera tripods stood like metal skeletons, their lenses unblinking, trained on the three figures seated at the centre.

Dr Mark sat in the middle, his posture straight but restrained. His face looked leaner than it had a week ago, as though sleep had abandoned him for days. On his right sat Meena, her hands folded tightly on the desk, eyes alert and protective. On his left was Ashok, unusually quiet.

A murmur rose as Mark drew forward and adjusted the microphone.

'As promised, I appear before you alive after lighting the lamp five days ago,' he said.

The room fell into instant silence.

Mark let his eyes travel across the crowd, across familiar faces from television screens and newspaper bylines. He took a slow breath.

'I did not come here to mock belief or to insult anyone's faith,' he continued, his voice steady but grave. 'I came because I nearly became another headline. Another photograph framed with garlands.'

A ripple of discomfort moved through the audience.

'I have found the reason why those who light the so called cursed lamp commit suicide,' Mark said. 'I experienced it myself, firsthand. I walked to the very edge of it.'

Meena glanced at him, but he did not look at her. His eyes remained fixed on the crowd.

'What the lamp does is not magic. It is not a spirit. It does not kill by fire or curse,' he said. 'It awakens something already buried inside the mind. Something unresolved. Something traumatic.'

A journalist raised his finger, but Mark lifted his palm, asking for patience.

'The people who died did not die because of the lamp,' he said. 'They died because the lamp triggered severe dissociative hallucinations. False memories. Guilt that was never real but felt absolute.'

Ashok shifted in his chair.

'When I lit that lamp, I began seeing my dead wife everywhere,' Mark said. 'Not as memory. As presence. As accusation. I believed I had committed a crime I never committed.'

The hall was completely still now.

'I was ready to end my life. Not because I feared the curse.

But because I believed I deserved punishment.'

Mark paused, allowing the words to settle.

'That is the danger,' he said quietly. 'Not the lamp. The mind.'

He leaned back slightly, his fingers resting on the table.

'The so called curse is nothing but psychological collapse triggered by suggestion, isolation and trauma. A perfect trap for vulnerable minds.'

A camera zoomed closer, catching the exhaustion in his eyes.

'I am alive because I questioned it in time,' Mark said. 'And because science arrived before superstition finished the job.'

Dr. Mark adjusted the microphone and waited for the restless murmur in the hall to settle. Rows of journalists inclined forward, pens poised, fingers hovering over record buttons.

'When I first examined this lamp, I made a conscious decision to forget every story associated with it. No folklore. No fear. No history of deaths. I approached it as a scientific anomaly. An object that had interacted with human biology in a consistent and deadly way.'

He gestured to the screen behind him, where images of the lamp appeared. Close-ups of the wick. The oil chamber. Cracks in the metal.

'This lamp is more than a hundred years old. Its oil is not just modern kerosene. It had presence of aged mixture of plant based oils that have undergone decades of chemical degradation. When such oils are burned, they do not merely produce light. They release vapours. Vapours that enter the lungs, pass into the bloodstream, and cross the blood brain barrier.'

The room fell silent.

'My team conducted detailed chemical analysis on the oil residue, the wick, the inner chamber and the metal casing. What we found explains everything.'

He lifted a document but did not open it.

'First, we detected Ergot Alkaloids. These compounds originate from fungi that grow on grains and plant oils stored in damp environments. Ergot Alkaloids are infamous. Chemically, they are closely related to substances that led to the synthesis of LSD. When burned and inhaled, they cause powerful hallucinations, altered perception of time and severe distortions of memory.'

Mark's eyes hardened.

'These compounds do not create fantasy. They distort reality. They pull fragments from your own mind and rearrange them into something that feels absolute and undeniable.'

A few journalists shifted uneasily.

'Second, we found Myristicin and Elemicin. These compounds are found in nutmeg oil, which was commonly used in old lamps as a fragrance and preservative. Inside the human body, these substances metabolise into chemicals that act similarly to MDMA and mescaline. They intensify emotions. Love becomes obsession. Guilt becomes unbearable. Fear becomes terror.'

He tapped the table lightly.

'Imagine experiencing the most painful memory of your life, magnified ten times, stripped of context, and replayed as if it is happening right now. That is what these compounds do.'

He took a breath.

'The lamp itself contributes further damage. Traces of Lead Oxide were found inside the chamber and paint. Lead poisoning is known to cause memory distortion, confusion, paranoia and emotional instability. Victims often cannot distinguish between past and present.'

Mark let that sink in.

'Mercury vapours were also present. Mercury was commonly used in antique metalwork. Inhaling mercury causes hallucinations, cognitive breakdown and emotional volatility. Historically, this condition was called Mad Hatter syndrome.'

A ripple of recognition moved through the room.

'We also detected Arsenic from antique pigments and dyes. Arsenic exposure causes delirium and vivid hallucinations. The brain enters a state where imagination and memory collapse into one.'

Mark's voice remained calm, almost cold.

'Additionally, inside the lamp, we found Stachybotrys. Toxic black mould. This mould produces mycotoxins that attack the nervous system. Symptoms include confusion, intrusive memories and neurological distress.'

He shifted forward slightly.

'There was more. Fungal contamination had grown deep within the lamp. Psilocybin like spores were present. When the lamp was lit, these spores burned and released psychoactive compounds directly into the air.'

A journalist whispered something to his colleague. Mark continued without pause.

'Now, let me explain what happens when a person lights this lamp.'

He raised his hand, counting on his fingers.

'The room is closed. There is no ventilation. The vapours build up rapidly. The person inhales a cocktail of hallucinogens, neurotoxins and heavy metals. Within minutes, the brain's emotional and memory centres are compromised.'

Mark touched his temple.

'The hippocampus, which governs memory, begins

to misfire. The amygdala, which processes fear and guilt, becomes hyperactive. The prefrontal cortex, responsible for rational thought, shuts down.'

He looked straight into the cameras.

'At this point, the brain fills the gaps. It creates a narrative. Not a dream. Not imagination. A memory.'

His voice lowered.

'A memory that feels completely real.'

Mark paused after the words for a moment.

'In my case, I believed I had murdered my own child. I could feel it. I could see it. I could smell it. I remembered it with absolute certainty.'

A hush swept the hall.

'That memory was a fabrication. A false narrative planted in my mind by chemical manipulation.'

He straightened.

'Every single person who lit this lamp likely experienced something similar. Their own worst fears. Their deepest guilt. Their unresolved trauma. Reshaped into horrific realities.'

Mark clenched his fist briefly, then relaxed it.

'When a human being is confronted with an unshakable memory of committing an unforgivable act, the mind collapses. Overwhelmed by fear and shame, they seek escape. And for many, that escape was death.'

He let the words hang.

'This is not possession. This is not a curse.'

Mark took a sip of water.

'There is something important I need everyone to understand.'

He leaned closer to the microphone.

'Memories are not like recorded videos on our smartphones, despite what people believe. They are not permanent files. Memories are chemical signals. Electrical patterns. Fragile and editable.'

His voice grew firmer.

'They can be manipulated even without external substances. Trauma does it. Fear does it. Suggestion does it. In this case, toxins invaded the brain and amplified the darkest corners of the subconscious.'

Mark glanced briefly at Meena and Ashok beside him, then back to the crowd.

'This lamp did not kill people by magic. It killed them by turning their own minds against them.'

He paused, allowing the weight of the statement to settle.

'Once we understood this, we recreated the exposure in controlled laboratory conditions using neurochemical simulations. The results were consistent. Hallucinations. False memory implantation. Emotional overload.'

Mark nodded slowly.

'The pattern matched every reported death.'

He lifted his head.

'The so called curse is nothing more than a psychological illusion reinforced by chemistry and coincidence.'

Mark's voice sharpened.

'And superstition did the rest.'

He straightened fully now.

The hall remained silent.

'This lamp is not haunted,' Mark said quietly. 'It never was.'

He looked into the lens of the nearest camera.

'It is a forgotten chemical trap, waiting patiently for its next victim.'

He stepped back from the microphone.

'Today, we end this story. Not with fear, but with understanding.'

The room erupted into questions, camera flashes and

raised voices. But Mark stood still, unmoved, as if he had finally put a ghost in a bottle.

*

The rain had softened into a gentle drizzle by evening, tapping against the windows of Mark's house. Ashok sat opposite Mark on the couch, legs crossed, arms folded, his expression hovering between irritation and relief. He had been staring at Mark for a while now, as if confirming that the man in front of him was real and intact.

'Of all the times in your life,' Ashok finally said, breaking the silence, 'you decided to light a suicidal lamp when I was not around.'

Mark smiled faintly. It was not a triumphant smile. It was the tired smile of someone who had returned from the edge.

'Bad timing,' Mark said, chuckling under his breath.

He reached for the pill bottle on the table, unscrewed the cap with practiced ease and took a tablet with a sip of water.

Ashok noticed.

'What's that pill for?' he asked.

'To keep my mind where it belongs,' Mark replied. 'To cure the frequent visions I have been having.'

'That's good,' he said. 'Those visions were making you weak in crucial situations. You know, I think you were already exhausted and traumatised by your wife's death. That grief must have made your mind more vulnerable to those false memories. With neurotoxins like these from that old lamp, creating hallucinations is usually easier than rewriting long-term memories. That part surprised me. You never emphasized that part at the press conference.'

'Because if I had,' Mark said quietly, 'the media would have started digging into the private lives of every victim. They would look for old wounds, past guilt, unfinished grief. They would turn those deaths into spectacles.'

He exhaled slowly.

'That would open a Pandora's box that cannot be closed again. I don't think the dead deserve that. Whatever their fears or secrets were, they should end with them. Not be dissected in public debates or primetime panels.'

Ashok's expression shifted as understanding settled in.

Mark turned his head.

'What's the update on your education?' he asked.

Ashok straightened a little, as if the question demanded formality.

'I have an exam tomorrow,' he said. 'I am rewriting a failed paper from the final semester. Used all these months away specifically to study and clear everything.'

Mark smiled, this time with genuine approval.

'That's great,' he said. 'Are you sure you dedicated all your time to studies?'

Ashok hesitated.

'Well, not exactly,' he said quickly. 'And do not shout at me.'

He drew forward, unlocked his phone and held it out to Mark. The screen glowed brightly.

A page loaded.

Dr Mark. Paranormal Investigator.

Mark raised an eyebrow.

'Already twenty thousand followers,' Ashok said proudly.

Mark took the phone, scrolling slowly. His name stared back at him, bold and definitive, followed by short clips, rational explanations and debunked myths.

'Did you get any messages or calls yet?' Mark asked.

'Plenty,' Ashok replied. 'Mostly AI generated supernatural videos. People genuinely believed them. I managed to explain most of it.'

Mark handed the phone back.

'Good,' he said.

Ashok was about to reply when his phone rang.

The screen flashed an unknown number.

He frowned and answered.

'Hello.'

Mark watched Ashok's expression change.

'Yes,' Ashok said. 'Yes, I am his assistant.'

He listened quietly, nodding once.

'Where?'

A pause.

'Theni? In Tamil Nadu?'

Mark sat upright.

'Okay,' Ashok said. 'I understand.'

The call ended.

Ashok looked at Mark, eyes bright with restrained excitement.

'Well, Dr Mark,' he said, 'it appears some people are convinced there is extraterrestrial alien activity in a rural village near Theni.'

Mark stared at him for a moment. Then he laughed. Not loudly, but deeply.

'Aliens,' Mark said. 'After ghosts and demons.'

He stood up slowly and walked to the window. The rain had almost stopped now. Clouds were parting, revealing a sliver of moonlight.

'Go write your exams,' Mark said without turning back. 'Prepare for your post graduation.'

Ashok opened his mouth to protest.

Mark raised a hand.

'There will be time in between,' he said calmly.

He turned to face Ashok.

'After the exam,' Mark continued, 'let us go catch some aliens.'

'YES!' Ashok punched the air in joy.

As the rain finally stopped, Mark knew that mysteries won't end. He has officially become a Paranormal Investigator now.

Acknowledgements

This book would not have taken its final shape without the guidance, patience and quiet support of several people who stood beside me in different ways during its creation.

My deepest gratitude goes to Dr Sreejith S.S., my cousin and Assistant Professor in the Department of Chemical Oceanography at CUSAT, Kerala. His expertise in coordination chemistry, crystallography, theoretical and DFT studies, and bioinorganic chemistry proved invaluable. He took the time to read the manuscript critically and offered precise feedback and corrections, ensuring that the scientific foundations of this story remained credible and grounded. In a narrative where realism is crucial, his guidance helped me avoid convenient shortcuts and strengthened the core of the book.

I owe a special thanks to my father, Vijayakrishnan, who suggested the name Markandeyan for the lead character, drawing inspiration from the Puranas. That single suggestion gave the character a deeper cultural resonance and an identity that stayed with me throughout the writing process.

I am grateful to Praveen Chandran, publisher and owner of Quantic Books, for believing in this project and for taking it forward with confidence. His support and trust made this book possible in its present form.

To my wife, Anjitha, I owe more than words can contain. This book was written alongside her patience, her quiet strength, and her unwavering emotional support. She lived with the moods of this story, the long hours, the distractions, and the doubts. If this book carries any emotional honesty, it is because she made space for it to exist.

Finally, I thank my family, Asha SP, Dr Sruthi Vijayakrishnan, and Deepu R.V. My mother, sister, and brother-in-law have been constant presences in my life, offering encouragement, reassurance and timely reminders to stay grounded.

This book belongs as much to them as it does to me.

ABOUT THE AUTHOR

Yadu Vijayakrishnan is a filmmaker, cinematographer and writer. At the age of 19, he worked as one of the cinematographers on the Brazilian film "Feio, Eu?" and subsequently made several short films before completing his graduation. He directed and produced over twenty historical documentaries and a fifty-episode travelogue series for a TV channel over two years.

Yadu directed the controversial documentary "21 Months of Hell," which portrayed the torture methods employed by the government during the Emergency period in India. Following this, he worked as the cinematographer for two films and directed two horror web series. He then directed the Sanskrit movie "Bhagavadajjukam," which had its world premiere at the International Film Festival of India and was screened at the Bangalore International Film Festival, BRICS Shanghai Film Festival, New York Indian Film Festival, Melbourne Indian Film Festival, Kolkata International Film Festival and Rajasthan International Film Festival.

Yadu Vijayakrishnan also served as an Advisory Panel Member of the Central Board of Film Certification under the Ministry of Information and Broadcasting, Government of India. He served as jury member for Indian Panorama, International Film Festival of India, Bangalore International Film Festival and IDPA (Indian Documentary Producers Association) Awards.

He is the son of National Award-winning film critic, director and writer Vijayakrishnan, and Asha (retired teacher). Yadu is married to Anjitha.

YADU'S PREVIOUS BOOKS

THE STORY OF AYODHYA
English - Novel
Historical/Political
grpr.in/tsa

VINES
English - Novel
Apocalyptic Thriller

ISRAEL:
ORU MAHAGATHA
Malayalam - Non-fiction
Historical

TALES OF
LORD SHIVA
English - Stories
Hinduism

INDIC
HORROR STORIES
English - Stories
Horror

To Order -

+91-8590 011 447

quanticcreatives.in
quanticcreatives@gmail.com